CW00859644

# LOVE'S REFLECTIONS

## LOVE'S MAGIC BOOK 4

## BETTY MCLAIN

Copyright (C) 2017 Betty McLain

Layout design and Copyright (C) 2019 by Creativia

Published 2019 by Creativia (www.creativia.org)

Edited by Marilyn Wagner

Cover art by Cover Mint

*This book is dedicated to everyone working to help make a better world by casting a reflection on our younger generation and teaching our young how to love. Love will always cast a good and meaningful reflection.*

# CHAPTER 1

Melanie smiled happily as she removed the sign from the door of the gallery and prepared to open for the day. The sign said "Closed for Valerie and Marcus' Wedding – Open Monday".

It had been a beautiful wedding and reception. Everyone enjoyed themselves, even after Valerie and Marcus left to start their much-anticipated honeymoon. Melanie sighed. They were so in love. It had been a joy to see her daughter so happy and in love. To think she owed it all to a bee. Melanie laughed softly. Marcus was a great addition to their family. Even though they were going to be living in Denton, they were close enough to visit regularly.

Melanie got everything ready for the new day. Angelica had asked for the day off to handle some business, which wasn't a problem, since the wedding was over. Melanie had more time for the gallery. When all was in order, Melanie went into the back to check in with Cindy.

"Good morning," she said, as she entered the back room.

"Good morning," replied Cindy. She looked up with a smile. "Did Valerie and Marcus get going okay?" she asked.

"Yes, they were so happy, I think they floated to the plane," replied Melanie, with a smile. She looked at the box Cindy was beginning to open. "Isn't that some of stuff we brought back from Italy?" asked Melanie, puzzled. "I thought all of the things we brought back were already taken care of and unpacked."

"This box must have gotten mixed in with some others. I just found it," replied Cindy.

Melanie looked on curiously, while Cindy opened the box. Cindy reached inside to withdraw an old-fashioned hand mirror. It was very clear. She turned it over and admired the intricate design on its back. It was very beautiful.

Melanie watched Cindy admire the mirror. She smiled as she saw how fascinated Cindy was with the mirror. "We bought those three mirrors from an old man in an antique store. He said the mirrors belonged to his three daughters. According to him, the daughters did not need the mirrors anymore. They are all happily married. The daughters only had sons so there were no daughters to pass the mirrors on to."

"I asked him if his daughter might want to hang on to the mirrors. He said 'no'. The mirrors had served their purpose, and it was time for them to help someone else."

"How can a hand mirror help anyone?" asked Cindy.

"I asked him the same question," said Melanie. "He said the mirrors will help someone find their true love. He said when a girl looks into the mirror, she will see a reflection of her true love looking back at her. The old man said it worked for his girls. Now it was time for someone else to be helped." Melanie stopped and smiled at Cindy. "I do not know if they work, but they were so beautiful, I had to buy all three."

Cindy dug into the box and unpacked the other two mirrors. She looked them over carefully. All three had different designs on them. One was silver-colored with large blue flowers on the back. She lay it down, carefully. The next mirror was copper-colored. It had a climbing yellow rose and a butterfly on its back. She lay it down and picked up the last mirror. It was gold-colored. It had some sort of shield on its back. She turned it around, slowly, to look in the glass. At first, she saw only her reflection looking back at her. As she kept looking, her reflection faded, and she saw the reflection of a man, standing at a bathroom mirror, shaving. He had soap over his face so she couldn't see his face plainly. Since he was without his shirt, she could see that he was very well put together. The man suddenly seemed to see her looking at him. He turned and looked behind him to see if there was anyone there in the room with him. When he saw there was no one behind him, he started to turn back to the mirror. Cindy quickly lay the mirror face down. Her cheeks flushed to think she had been spying on someone in their bathroom.

"How much are you going to ask for the mirrors?" she asked Melanie.

Melanie had been watching Cindy with the gold mirror. She wondered who Cindy had seen in the mirror. She smiled. She would just have to be patient and see what happened. "I'm not going to sell them," replied Melanie. "I want to display one of them in the gallery. I want a large sign behind it saying, 'Look in the Mirror to Find Your True Love'. It should be a great draw for the gallery." Melanie smiled as she waited for Cindy's reaction.

"Yes, it will," agreed Cindy. "I'll get it set up." She picked up the gold mirror. When she looked in it, it showed only her reflection. "If you think of a price, I want this one. It feels like it should be mine."

Melanie smiled at Cindy. "You may have it," she said. "Who knows, it might show you the person who is meant for you."

Cindy smiled as she hugged the mirror to her chest. "Who knows? Stranger things have happened. Thanks, Melanie."

Melanie went out to the front to wait for customers. Cindy went to put up her mirror and to design a display for the front room of the gallery. While she was working, her mind drifted back to the hunk she saw in the mirror. Even with soap on his face, she could tell he was very nice to look at.

Cindy thought about the story the old man told Melanie. Was it possible the man she saw in the mirror was her own true love? Cindy grinned. Then her grin faded. How was she supposed to get together with her hunk? She had no idea who he was.

# CHAPTER 2

Officer James Michaels looked in the mirror as he finished shaving. He knew he had seen a lovely young lady in the mirror. Where had she come from? Where had she gone? Was she a ghost? Was the house haunted? Was there a ghost watching him shave? He had never seen any sign of a ghost before. Maybe it was his imagination. If he had to pick a girl to fantasize about, he sure picked a looker. He grinned as he dressed in his uniform and prepared for another work day.

He would be spending part of it in court, testifying. He had to hurry. It was never good to keep the Court waiting. After court, he would be on patrol. There would be a new recruit joining him as a ride-along trainee. The trainee was newly graduated from the police academy. Officer Michaels was to be his trainer and show him what would be expected of him as a police officer. Hopefully he could teach the new cadet how to stay out of trouble on the streets of the city.

When he came out of the courthouse, the new cadet was waiting for him by his car. The cadet smiled and offered his hand. Officer Michaels noticed the cadet had the look of a Native American about him.

"I'm Mark Black Feather. I understand you are to be my training officer," the young cadet said.

"I'm Officer James Michaels. I didn't know I would be training a Native American," replied Officer Michaels, shaking the young cadet's hand.

"Is that a problem?" asked Mark Black Feather, his smile fading.

"No," Officer Michaels responded. "I just thought most Native American graduates joined the police force on the reservation."

"Yes," said Mark. "Most do join the reservation force, but I wanted to get more experience before deciding where I belong."

"It's good to know a bit about life before settling down. How old are you?" he asked. The young man did not look old enough to be a graduate.

"I'm 23," replied Mark. "How old are you?"

"I'm 34," replied Officer Michaels. "Let's get on the road." He motioned for Mark to take the passenger seat as he took the driver's seat.

"Where do we patrol?" asked Mark.

"I have a route I cover every day. I try to vary the times so I can catch law-breakers by surprise. These are rough streets. There will be drug pushers, gang members, and prostitutes. You have to be very careful, and watch your back. You also have to earn their respect. If you do not earn their respect, they will run right over you." Officer Michaels ended his warning speech as he turned onto the road through the park.

"Is this the park where Angelica Black was found?" asked Mark, Looking around curiously.

"Yes," replied Officer Michaels. "I'm the one who found her."

Mark looked over at him excitedly. "Is she as beautiful as everyone says?" he asked.

"She is very nice looking," replied Officer Michaels, absentmindedly. His mind went back to the face in the mirror. He shook his head to clear his thoughts, to focus on the present and his conversation with his new recruit.

"You've never met Miss Black?" he asked.

"No," Mark replied. "I was already at the academy when she returned."

"Returned from where?" asked Officer Michaels.

Mark paused for a moment before answering. "I don't know. She went away for a while after the death of her parents," Mark replied.

Officer Michaels shrugged, losing interest in the conversation. He was looking at someone across the park.

Mark looked over to where Officer Michaels was watching. There was a group of older boys around two younger boys. The older boys were taunting the younger boys. As they watched, one of the older boys shoved one of the younger ones. The young boy fell. His friend helped him to stand and they faced the older boys defiantly.

Officer Michaels eased out of the patrol car and closed the door quietly, so that the boys would not hear the door close. He started to walk across the park toward the boys. Mark followed his example and eased out of the car, closing his door quietly. He started to cross the park also, but at an angle, so he would be behind the boys.

"Leave us alone," one of the younger boys told the older boys, defiantly.

The older boys just laughed at them, and one of the boys reached out to shove him again. One of the older boys looked up and spotted Officer Michaels almost reaching their group. He turned and started to run.

"Freeze," said Officer Michaels in a loud, stern voice.

All of the boys turned and looked toward Officer Michaels. One of the boys, in the group, swaggered forward.

"Hello, David," said Officer Michaels. "Up to your old tricks, I see."

"What are you going to do about it?" scoffed the teen. "You know you can't take me in. My dad would have your badge."

Officer Michaels looked at the boys sternly. "I told you boys, the last time I caught you bullying the younger boys, what would happen to you if I caught you again. I guess you did not listen, or you did not believe me. I talked to your father about the situation, David. He told me to use my own judgment. He said talking to you was getting him nowhere. You ignored him. He is tired of getting complaints about your behavior."

David looked at him shocked. "I don't believe you. You are just trying to scare me!" David exclaimed.

While the boys focused on Officer Michaels, Mark came up behind them. One of the boys had a large rock in his hand. He was hiding his hand so the rock would not be seen. When he raised his hand and tossed the rock, Mark tackled him. He yelled at the same time to warn Officer Michaels.

Officer Michaels dodged the rock and walked over to where Mark had the boy on the ground.

"Cuff him," he said. "All of you are going downtown."

Officer Michaels pushed the radio speaker on his shoulder and spoke to the dispatcher. "I need pickup in the park for six teens," he said after giving his badge number.

"It's on the way," the dispatcher said. "What's the charge?"

"Assaulting a police officer, accessory, and public disturbance," replied Officer Michaels.

"You can't charge all of us," exclaimed David. "We didn't know he was going to throw a rock."

"It doesn't matter. You were all together, so you are all accessories. You are all going in."

The police van pulled to a halt in the park. Four policemen got out and headed across the park toward the group.

"Hi, James," said the first policeman to reach them. "What's up?"

"Hello, Eric," said Officer Michaels. "David and his friends here were creating a public disturbance by bullying these two youngsters. Then the one in handcuffs decided to add assaulting a police officer to their crimes by throwing a large rock at me. The other boys are charged as accessories. They need to see what happens when they break the law. They need to see what a cell looks and feels like."

Eric turned to the other policemen. "Cuff them and load them up," he instructed.

The policemen hurried to follow his instructions. They handcuffed the boys and escorted them toward the van.

"Thanks, Eric," said Officer Michaels. "I'll catch up on the paperwork when I finish my patrol."

"Anytime," responded Eric. "This your new trainee?" he asked motioning at Mark.

"Yes, he saved me from getting bashed with a rock. Mark Black Feather, meet Eric Collin." The two of them exchanged greetings and handshakes.

"Good job, Mark," said Eric.

"Thanks," replied Mark.

"I'll see you later, James," said Eric, with a wave, as he went to join his men.

After the van left, Officer Michaels turned to the two youngsters. They had been watching everything with wide eyed fascination.

"Are you boys alright?" asked Officer Michaels.

One of the boys grinned up at him. "We are fine now," he replied. "David was mad because my Dad told him to stay away from my sister. He told him he didn't want a young hoodlum around his family. David was very mad,"

"You have a smart Dad. You boys head on home now, and tell your Dad what happened. Tell him David probably won't be locked up for long, and to watch out for him."

"I will, thanks, Officer Michaels. I'm glad you showed up when you did," said the boy. The other boy smiled and added his thanks, as they turned and headed for home.

Officer Michaels turned to Mark and grinned. "Thanks for saving me from our rock thrower. Are you ready to go back on patrol?"

"You're welcome. I don't think being your trainee is going to be boring," Mark replied, as they headed for the patrol car.

When they reached the patrol car, Officer Michaels pulled out his cell phone and dialed a number. The call was answered after the first ring. "Hello, Mayor's Office," answered a voice.

"Hello, Joanie. This is Officer James Michaels. Is the mayor in?"

"Yes, hold a minute, Officer Michaels," she replied.

"Hello," answered the mayor.

"Hello, Mr. Mayor. This is Officer James Michaels. I just arrested David and five of his friends for public disturbance and as accessory in the attack on a police officer. They were in the park bullying a couple of young boys because the boy's father had told David to stay away from his daughter. One of the boys decided to throw a rock at me."

The Mayor sighed loudly. "Are you alright?'

"I'm fine. My partner stopped him."

"Good, Thanks for letting me know. I'll take care of it," replied the Mayor.

"Could you wait a couple of hours before getting him out? If you could, talk to some of the other boys' parents, also. I think it will do the boys good to sweat it out for a while. It might make them stop and think about the direction they are headed. I'll talk to the Judge and see if he will give them community service. They won't feel like they got off scot free. Maybe this will be a wake-up call to these youngsters. If we don't stop them now, they are likely to end up in a gang, or in prison." Officer Michaels waited for the mayor's response.

"Alright, I'll call around and see what I can do. Thanks for trying to help. All of our talking hasn't sunk in with these boys. I don't want my son to end up a criminal or in a gang. Maybe we can finally figure out a way to get through to them."

"I hope so, Mr. Mayor," said Officer Michaels as they both said goodbye and hung up their phones.

Officer Michaels started the patrol car and continued on his route. He noticed Mark giving him curious sideways glances. "Being an officer doesn't just mean throwing people in jail. Sometimes, Its about helping to keep kids out of jail and giving them a chance to do better," he explained.

"You sound just like Moon Walking," commented Mark.

"Moon Walking? Isn't she an elder on the reservation?"

"Yes, she keeps everyone one their toes. She is always saying things like you just said," Mark smiled.

"She sounds like a very smart lady," remarked Officer Michaels.

"She is," agreed Mark.

There were no more incidents on their patrol. They

arrived back at the station in good time and went inside to deal with paperwork.

They met some of the boys leaving as they entered the station house. They were in the custody of their fathers. Each father stopped and shook Officer Michaels' hand. They all apologized for the trouble their boys caused and thanked him for his help. The boys looked on in astonishment at their fathers' actions. It was a valuable lesson for the boys.

The officers finished the paperwork, and calling goodbye to the other officers in the station house, exited the building. They stopped beside the patrol car. "Do you need a lift?" asked Officer Michaels.

"No, I have my car," said Mark.

"Ok, I'll see you in the morning. Good night," said Officer Michaels, as he turned and opened his door. A reflection in the glass caught his eye, but it was gone in a blink.

"Just my imagination," mumbled Officer Michaels.

# CHAPTER 3

Cindy stood back and studied the display she just finished designing for the silver mirror. She had built a frame and covered it with black velvet. The mirror was in the center, attached with a wire around it. The wire went through the velvet and was tied behind the frame. There was a sign at the bottom. In large words it said "LOOK IN THE MIRROR" Then under those words, in smaller letters it said "Some will see their true love looking back. (Will it be YOU?)"

Melanie finished with a customer and came over to look. She studied the sign.

"I like it," she said. "This should create a sensation."

Cindy grinned. "As soon as word gets around, there will be a lot of girls here trying out the mirror."

"I'm counting on it. This could get interesting," she smiled at Cindy and patted her arm. "Good job." Melanie went to help a new customer and Cindy returned to the back room.

"We should have quite a bit of excitement around here as soon as word gets out about the mirror. Even the unbelievers will have to come and check it out," Cindy murmured on the way to clean away her tools and straighten up. She put everything away, and gathering her belongings and her new mirror, she called good night to Melanie as she headed for home.

Melanie smiled as she watched Cindy leave. She saw the mirror Cindy was clutching and wondered just who Cindy had seen in the mirror earlier.

Cindy carefully lay the mirror on the passenger seat. She then changed her mind and picked it up again and gazed into the glass. Her own reflection stared back at her. She lay the mirror back on the seat and, starting the car, headed for home.

Cindy splurged the year before and put a down payment on a nice, two-bedroomed house. It may have seemed a bit much for a single woman, such as herself, but she was tired of living in an apartment. She wanted a home, something small, cozy, and all hers. She unlocked and entered the front. She dropped her keys in a bowl, on the table, just inside the front door. Cindy hung her coat in the closet and took her purse and mirror with her into the kitchen. She lay the purse and mirror on the dining table, then went to check the refrigerator to see what looked edible.

"I guess I'll have a salad," she murmured. Cindy took out lettuce, tomatoes, purple onion, olives, carrots, and a bottle of ranch dressing. She dumped everything on the cabinet, and took down a large bowl to mix it in. After washing everything, she began slicing and dicing. She put everything in the bowl, as she finished preparing the items. After sprinkling salt and bacon bits on the salad, she added the dressing and tossed all of the ingredients to mix them up.

"Umm, that looks good," said Cindy.

She carried the bowl and a plate to the table. After getting a fork, Cindy sat down to enjoy her salad. After she had eaten about half of her salad, Cindy looked down the table where she had left the mirror. After a few moments, she rose from her chair and went to get the it. She sat back at the table and studied it closely as she continued eating.She looked at the badge on the back of the mirror. It did not have any words on it, and she did not know what type of badge it was, but it looked good on the golden background. She turned the mirror around and looked in the glass.

"Oh my," said Cindy, softly. There was a reflection of two policemen in the window of a patrol car. The man from this morning was talking to a Native American policeman. "My guy is a policeman," she said, softly.

The reflection faded as he opened the car door. Cindy sighed, and lay the mirror on the table, face up. She wanted to keep an eye on it. She did not want to miss another chance to see her policeman.

Cindy finished the salad on her plate. She put the leftovers in a bowl with a tight lid and put the bowl in the refrigerator. She took her plate and fork to the sink and washed them. After drying them, she put them away.

Cindy grabbed her purse and mirror and headed for the bedroom, unbuttoning her blouse as she went. She lay her purse and the mirror on her dresser, while she finished undressing and gathering up a robe before heading to the shower. When she came out, she grabbed the TV remote and the mirror. She crawled onto the bed and lay back comfortably. She surfed through the channels but did not find anything interesting to watch, so she turned the TV off. Cindy picked up the mirror and looked into it again. She sighed. She was becoming obsessed with the mirror.

She was about to lay the mirror down, when her policeman appeared in it again. He looked like he was just arriving home. There was a mirror in his entrance hallway. He was looking down as he emptied his pockets. He started to turn and go into the room when something caught his eye, and he glanced up into the mirror.

He stopped and stared as he saw the same woman he had seen in the bathroom mirror. They stared at each other for a minute. Then, he smiled at the reflection. Cindy smiled back.

"Are you a ghost?" he asked.

Cindy shook her head. "No, she replied. "I'm looking in a magic mirror."

"Where did you get a magic mirror?" he asked.

"My employer brought it back from Italy," she replied.

"I didn't know such things existed," he observed.

"I didn't either until this morning," said Cindy.

"Not that I am bashful or anything, but how long were you watching in the bathroom this morning?" he asked with a smile.

Cindy blushed and ducked her head.

"Just for a minute," she said. "I only saw you with soap all over your face." He smiled at her. "I saw you earlier as you were leaving the police station. You were with a Native American policeman."

"He is my new trainee. His name is Mark. My name is James."

"My name is Cindy."

"It's nice to meet you, Cindy. It's a little weird meeting someone through a mirror," said James.

"Yes, it is," agreed Cindy.

The mirror suddenly reverted to her own reflections. "Well," said Cindy. "I guess we lost our connection. I hope it's not permanent. I did not get his last name or tell him mine." She relaxed back with a sigh. "I got to talk to my hunk," she said.

James was startled as Cindy's face disappeared from his mirror. He stared at it for a minute to see if Cindy's reflection would return. After a while he resigned himself to the fact that it would not come back and continued into the kitchen to eat. He had stopped and picked up some burgers and fries on the way home. They smelled very good to his hungry stomach. He smiled at the thought of Cindy. He felt lucky that his first experience with magic had found him a face of a beauty.

"I sure hope I get to see more of her," he said. "I did not get her last name. I don't even know if she lives in Rolling Fork. She could be anywhere."

James finished eating and cleaned up after himself. He went to take a shower and got into some more comfortable clothes. With a moment's pause, he pinned a towel up over the bathroom mirror. He wanted to see the woman again, but preferably when he had clothes on. After showering and dressing, he went into the living room and turned on the TV. He couldn't find anything to watch, so he left it on a talk show. He was not really paying attention. All he could think about was Cindy. He wanted to know more about her. He felt a strong pull between the two of them. He had never felt this kind of draw for any other person. It felt like they were already connected. They were supposed to be important to each other. He could only hope Cindy felt the same connection.

# CHAPTER 4

*C*indy went into work the next morning with a sense of excitement. She was waiting to see what would happen with the mirror display. She was still thinking about her conversation with James. Her mirror was hugged close to her chest, as she opened the back door of the gallery and prepared for a new day.

Cindy put away her purse and, after a long look in her mirror, she put the it with her purse. She put coffee on to brew for when Melanie and Frank arrived. While the coffee was brewing, Cindy went to the front room to check on the display and to make sure everything was in order. She had just finished, and gone back into the break room, when Melanie and Frank entered by the back door. Cindy poured two cups of coffee and had them waiting for Melanie and Frank when they entered the break room.

"Good morning," she said, handing each a cup of coffee.

"Good morning, you are a lifesaver," said Melanie. "Are you ready for the big day?"

"What big day?" Frank asked.

"We are showing our new mirror display this morning. It's sure to draw a lot of attention," remarked Melanie.

Frank grinned and smiled at Cindy. "We have to stay out of the way. When those girls find out about the magic mirror, they will run over everyone to have a look," he said. Cindy smiled back, but she didn't say anything.

Melanie turned to Frank and gave him a hug. "You just stay in your office. I'll protect you," she teased.

Frank returned her hug and turned to go to his office. "Thanks for the coffee, Cindy," he said, as he left. Cindy smiled and nodded her head.

"Well," repeated Melanie. "Are you excited about the new display?"

"Yes," agreed Cindy. "I have a feeling we are about to make history in this town."

"I certainly hope so. I like to keep everyone on their toes. Makes life much more interesting," Melanie rubbed her hands together and smiled at Cindy.

After Melanie went to the front to open the store, Cindy got down some boxes and started sorting stock and unpacking. She logged and kept a list of everything as she unpacked and was quickly absorbed in what she was doing. After a couple of hours, she heard loud talking from the front of the gallery. Cindy grinned as she put down her tools and headed for the front room. There was a group of girls crowded around the mirror. Cindy watched and listened for a few minutes.

"I don't think it works," said one of the girls. "It must be a joke."

Cindy came forward into the group. "You are all confusing the mirror," she remarked. "The mirror doesn't know who to show. You need to look one at a time. If your true love is not around something showing his reflection, you won't see him. You will have to keep trying until everything is in its proper place. Now, one at a time, line up and look in the mirror."

The girls made a line and came forward one at a time to look in the mirror. The first three looked and went to the side to wait on their friends. They were plainly disappointed. The fourth girl stepped up to look in the mirror. She drew a deep breath and smiled a big smile. She stood staring into the mirror for a few minutes. Finally, the next girl in line demanded her turn.

"Come on, Mari," she said. "We want to look, too."

Mari turned, with a happy smile, and moved out of line.

"Did you see someone in the mirror?" asked one of the other girls.

"Yes," Mari answered. "It was someone I met a couple of weeks ago. I liked him, and I thought he liked me, too. There was a strange connection between us. Now, I know why I was so drawn to him. He is my true love."

The other girls quickly went through and looked in the mirror. No one else seemed to see anyone. Cindy watched the girls and, when they had all had a turn, she told them they were welcome to come back anytime and check again. Cindy and Melanie watched the girls leave. They were all talking to Mari and questioning her about her guy. Melanie looked at Cindy.

"You handled them very well. How did you know they needed to go one at a time?" asked Melanie.

"It just seemed to make sense," Cindy shrugged. "I had better get back to work." Cindy headed for the stock room. She made a stop on the way, in the break room. She wanted a quick glance in her mirror. Cindy looked in her mirror and sighed with disappointment. There was only her image in the mirror. She put the mirror up and went to work.

"I'll have to try again later," she mused.

The next three days passed by much like the first. There was a continuous stream of girls coming to look in the mirror.

Cindy caught glimpses of James and Mark, as they went around town on patrol. She would see them when they passed windows or other reflective objects. She thought James may have caught a glimpse of her a couple of times, but she couldn't be sure. The reflections did not last long each time. They faded very quickly.

"It's like the mirror is playing with us," said Cindy.

Cindy went to the front to work on a new display she was designing. She said "Hi," to Angelica. Melanie was taking the day off.

"When are you and Alex getting married?" she asked Angelica.

"It's all set up for two weeks from now," said Angelica smiling happily as she rang up her customer. "You are coming, aren't you? You can bring a guest with you. It's going to be on the reservation. Moon Walking is in charge of all of the arrangements. Will you be able to come?"

"I would love to come. I'll have to let you know about the guest, but I'll definitely be there."

"Good," replied Angelica. "The mirror display has been a big attraction. I think almost every female in town, even the married ones, has been by to look in it. Only a few have seen anyone besides themselves in the mirror. They keep trying, though. I guess everyone wants to believe in true love."

"Yes, it is most people's eternal hope. It's sad when they give up looking and settle. They never get to experience the special connection of true love, like you and Alex," said Cindy.

"Yes, it is sad. We are very lucky. I am so grateful the universe decided we belonged together," said Angelica.

A customer came in and Angelica went to help her while Cindy worked on preparing a new display.

# CHAPTER 5

*J*ames and Mark parked the patrol car and walked down the street in the warehouse district. They had not seen anything wrong, but James wanted the people around the streets to know he was keeping an eye on things.

He had not seen Cindy again except for brief glimpses in windows every now and then. He wished he knew her last name. He could have looked her up. He was very intrigued by her. James shook his head. He needed to get his mind off of Cindy and back on the job.

Mark was working out very well. He followed orders well and quickly. He was smart, and when he voiced his opinion, he was worth listening to. He was willing to listen and learn. He was a good partner to have and good for the company.

"Why don't we head back to the car and head out for lunch?" James remarked.

"Fine by me," Mark replied.

They turned and crossed the street. On the other side of the street, they headed back toward the patrol car. As they came level with an alley, James heard voices. He held up a hand as a signal for Mark to stop. They both drew their weapons and eased into the alley. They walked, slowly, down the alley. James eased around a large garbage container. On the other side of the container was a tent made out of a blanket. Some more blankets were inside the tent, and there was a man and a young boy sitting inside the tent on the blankets. They looked startled and afraid when they saw two policeman pointing guns at them.

"We haven't done anything wrong," said the man.

Mark and James put away their guns.

"Who are you and what are you doing here?" asked James.

"I'm Greg Perkins and this is my son Bobby. We are temporarily down on our luck," said Greg.

"Do you have any identification," asked James.

"Yes," responded Greg, taking out his wallet and handing his driver's license to James. James looked at the license and the smiling picture of Greg and Bobby and a young woman in the wallet.

"Is this your wife?" he asked.

"Yes," responded Greg. He ducked his head and swallowed hard. "She passed on a month ago. She had an aneurysm. It took all of my savings for the funeral. I had to take time off to take care of everything, and my boss told me he no longer needed me."

"I see," said James. "You know you cannot stay here. It is not safe for Bobby. You are also trespassing."

"I know. I have been looking for somewhere else for us to live. We had to move out of the house we were in. It went with the job. When the job went, the house went, too," Greg sighed despondently.

James stood thinking. "If I might make a suggestion," said Mark. James looked at Mark.

"Sure," he said. "Go ahead."

"The Black Foundation is renovating a lot of houses. They just bought them and they were in bad shape. They may be able to help," he said.

"How do we get in touch with them?" asked James.

Mark took out his phone and dialed a number. It rang three times before it was answered.

"Hello, Mark," said Moon Walking. "You may take the man and his son to the art gallery. Angelica will take care of them."

"Thanks, Moon Walking," said Mark.

"Feed them first. The boy is hungry," said Moon Walking.

"Yes, I will. Thanks again, Moon Walking." They both hung up.

"Moon Walking said to take them to Angelica Black at the art gallery. She said Angelica will take care of them. Oh, she said to feed them first. She said Bobby is hungry."

"You did not even ask her anything," remarked James.

Mark laughed. "You do not have to explain things to Moon Walking. She already knows."

James looked puzzled. "I guess so. Are you hungry Bobby?" Bobby nodded his head shyly. "Alright, we were about to go on lunch break anyway. Why don't you help Greg gather their belongings and I will go fetch the car?" James told Mark.

James left to get the car and Mark and Greg gathered up the few toys, clothes, and blankets. They rolled everything into one of the blankets, only leaving out a toy bear for Bobby.

When James returned with the car, He popped open the trunk and Greg put the bundle inside. Greg and Bobby climbed inside the back seat. James looked into the back seat and shook his head. He popped open the trunk rummaged around and came up with a child seat. He brought it around and had Bobby get out while he installed the seat for him to sit in. He then put Bobby into the seat and buckled him in.

"All set," he smiled at Bobby. "Now we can go eat." Bobby smiled and nodded.

James and Mark climbed into the car and they drove to a nearby Burger King. They all piled out. Greg helped Bobby out and held onto his hand as they went inside.

"You all get a table while I order," James told Mark. Mark nodded agreement and led the way to an empty table. James was soon back with burgers and fries for everyone. He had a chocolate shake for Bobby and gave empty cups to Mark and Greg for their drinks. He stayed with Bobby and helped him get ready to eat, while they went for drinks. After they returned, he went to get his drink.

Everyone ate quietly. Greg and Bobby gobbled their food down. He could tell they had been skipping meals. "What is the name of the company you were employed at?" he asked Greg.

"Lamar Industries," he answered. "They make car engine parts. I had been with them for three years. I had no idea they treated people this way."

"With some companies it is all about the bottom line. People are expendable to them," remarked James.

They all finished their food. James ordered two more burgers and fries to take with them. He handed the bag to Greg when they were all seated and buckled in.

"Thanks," said Greg.

"No problem," said James with a shrug.

"Okay, if everyone is ready, we'll head over to the gallery to see Miss Black," said James as he started the car.

James parked the patrol car in front of the gallery and

they all went inside. Angelica came forward to greet them. Melanie was working the cash register.

"Hello, Officer Michaels," she greeted with a smile.

"Hello, Miss Black. Please call me James."

"Only, if you call me Angelica. I'm not going to be Miss Black much longer, anyway. Alex and I are getting married in two weeks," she replied

"Congratulations, I hope you both will be very happy," he motioned to Mark. "This is my partner Mark Black Feather and the other two are Greg and Bobby Perkins. They are who we came to see you about."

"Yes, I know. Moon Walking filled me in." Angelica nodded to Mark and Greg, and then she knelt down in front of Bobby and offered him her hand. Bobby shyly put his hand in hers. "Hello, Bobby," she said. "I'm glad Moon Walking sent you to me."

"Greg, I need to talk to you about where to send you," she said rising and facing Greg.

"What do you mean?" asked Greg.

"Well, I can set you up in a house, but without a job, or someone to watch Bobby, you will have a hard time of it. I also have another option. Have you ever done any yard work?"

"Yes, I worked part time for a landscaping company before starting my last job," he replied.

"Would you consider yard work again? I have a large estate. You wouldn't be doing all the work by yourself. There are three other day workers. They do not live on the estate. I also have a fully furnished house you can move into. It will come with the job, along with a salary. I also have a house keeper and a helper working in the house. They both have small children and could help out with Bobby. Do you think you would be interested in working for me?"

"Oh, yeah!" Greg exclaimed beaming from ear to ear.

"Good, give me a few minutes and I'll take you both home," Angelica turned to tell Melanie she was leaving.

James gave Mark his keys and told him to get Greg's things out of the trunk. "Oh, don't forget the car seat. He will need it," James added. With that taken care of, he casually wandered over to the other side of the room. James had noticed a line of girls in front of a display and was curious what they could be looking at. He was surprised to see a mirror with a sign in front of it saying something about seeing your true love in the mirror.

While he was watching the mirror and the girls, Angelica appeared beside him. "It doesn't work for guys only girls," she said with a smile.

James was quietly working things out in his head. Cindy said she was looking in a magic mirror. She said her employer brought it back from Italy. True love, he thought, smiling. He turned to Angelica.

"Is Cindy here?" he asked.

Angelica looked surprised. "No, she had a dental appointment. She won't be back today," she replied.

"Thank you for helping out with Greg and Bobby," he said, having all the info he needed.

"I'm happy to help. Besides I have my orders from Moon Walking. She told me it was important to take very good care of Bobby and his Dad."

"What did she mean by that?" asked James.

"I don't know, but if Moon Walking says it is important, I know it is. I'll see you later, James." Angelica walked towards the door and, with a last look at the mirror, James followed.

James had a big grin on his face when he got to the car. He told Greg and Bobby goodbye and wished them well. He couldn't seem to stop smiling as he thought about Cindy. He knew how to find her. He noticed Mark giving him puzzling looks. "What is it?" he asked.

"I don't think I have ever noticed you being so happy," Mark replied.

"I have a right to be happy," said James. "I think I have found the girl of my dreams," he replied.

"I am happy for you, but when did you find her? I have been with you all day and I haven't seen any girls, except Miss Black, and she is spoken for," remarked Mark.

James laughed. "It is not Miss Black. You will just have to wait and see," replied James with a big smile.

# CHAPTER 6

Cindy went home after her dental checkup. She had the next two days off. She couldn't stop thinking about James. She had no idea how close she had been to meeting him in person. She took out her mirror as soon as she entered her house. The mirror showed only her reflection. There was not even a hint of James' reflection. She sighed and lay down the mirror. She may as well get started on her chores. The first thing to do was make a grocery list. She could get her grocery shopping done. It would be one less thing to do on her days off.

Cindy headed for the kitchen with a pen and some paper. She sat at the table and started her list. When she was about halfway through, the phone rang. Cindy hurried back to the front, where she had left her purse and dug out her phone. "Hello," she said.

"Hi, Cindy," said Angelica. "I was wondering if you know Officer James Michaels. He brought a man and his little boy by the gallery for me to help today. While he was there, he asked if you were there. I told him you were at the dentist. I thought I should check with you about him. I hope it was alright for me to tell him."

Cindy started grinning. "Yes, I know him. It is fine. Did you get everything settled with the man and his son?"

"Yes," said Angelica. "They are all settled in. He is going to work on the grounds. Moon Walking said it was important to help him and his son."

"Since Moon Walking said it, they are right where they need to be. No one would argue with her," Cindy said with a laugh.

"I know. I am very glad she is in my life. In two weeks she will be my Grandmother. I feel like she is already my Grandmother. I think she is the whole tribe's grandmother. She takes care of all of us. We are blessed to have her." Angelica finished with a laugh.

"Yes, we all are," agreed Cindy.

"Well, I'll let you go. Enjoy your days off," said Angelica.

"I will," agreed Cindy.

They both hung up and Cindy did a little happy dance. "My guy found me. His name is Officer James Michaels, and he lives in Rolling Fork." She danced around some more. "I had better get this list finished and my shopping done. If I hear from him, I don't want to be tied up with chores."

Cindy finished her list and grabbed her keys. She started walking out of the door and stopped. She went back for her purse and phone. She was so excited; she almost forgot to lock her door.

Cindy sailed through her shopping in a fog. Somehow, she managed to get everything on her list and get back home safely. She unloaded her groceries and began putting everything away. When she was finished, the house received a quick dusting and straightening. It wasn't very dirty. She tended to put things where they belonged when she used them and she was the only one there.

Cindy finished all of her chores in record time. She was too excited to sit down. She took up her mirror and gazed into it. She was thrilled to see James and Mark at the park. They were reflected in a small pool of water. They were both gazing into the water looking for something.

Mark suddenly pointed at something and hurried around the water and, reaching in, pulled a small kitten from the water. He brought the dripping, shivering bundle back around to James.

A mother, with a small child in a stroller, handed him a towel to wrap the kitten in. She had been the one to tell them about seeing some boys throw something in the water.

James rubbed the kitten and wrapped him up. The boys had tied the kitten's front legs together, so he untied the front legs and handed him back to Mark. He turned to talk to the mother.

She gave him a description of the boys, and he thanked her for her help. When he started to turn away from the pond, he saw Cindy's reflection in the pond. He started smiling, but he hardly had time to see her before her reflection faded.

Cindy sat back, disappointed not to have had more interaction with James. Then, she started smiling. She knew who he was now, and he knew who she was. They were bound to meet face to face, soon.

James and Mark took the kitten to the animal shelter. They wanted it checked out before they tried to find a home for it. The best vet in town worked at the animal shelter.

"Hi, James," said Dr. Stanley Dark. "What have you got for me today?"

"Hi, Stanley," returned James. "Some boys tried to drown this kitten. I thought you could give him a check and see if he has any problems." Stanley took the small bundle from Mark. "This is my new trainee, Mark Black Feather. Mark this is Dr. Stanley Dark. He is the best vet around." said James.

Stanley grinned at James. "I'm the only vet you know. Nice to meet you, Mark. Tell Moon Walking I said 'hello' next time you see her. She is an inspiration to us all," Stanley grinned at Mark.

"I will be sure to tell her," said Mark.

Stanley had been looking over the kitten while he talked. He now turned to James. "The kitten is fine. You want me to give him his shots?"

"Yes," said James. James waited while Stanley gave the kitten his shots.

"Do you know anyone who might be interested in adopting a kitten," he asked Stanley.

"No, but, if you take him to Moon Walking, she is sure to know just where to take him. I would not be surprised to know she probably already has a home picked out for him." Stanley and Mark laughed at this observation.

James picked up the small kitten. The kitten purred and reaching up licked his chin. "Okay, small stuff, are you ready for a ride?"

The kitten purred in agreement.

# CHAPTER 7

*J*ames gave the kitten to Mark to hold while he was driving. He was just starting the car when the phone rang. "Hello," said James.

"Hello, James, this is Angelica Black. Moon Walking told me you have a kitten for Bobby. I'll be at Carson's Grocery in about fifteen minutes. I need to pick up a few things for the kitten. If you can meet me there, it will save you a trip out here."

"Fine, we will meet you at Carson's Grocery in fifteen minutes."

James hung up the phone and Mark looked at him curiously.

"We will be meeting Angelica to give her the kitten. It seems Moon Walking has decided Bobby needs a pet," said James.

Mark burst out laughing. After a minute, James joined him. "Moon Walking is always a step ahead," said Mark.

They drove by the park on the way to the store. Everything looked quiet. Most of the children had left the park for the day. The few who were left were starting to leave. James and Mark kept an eye on the stragglers for a little while, as they left the park. James drove on to meet Angelica.

Angelica came out of the store as they drove up and stopped. Mark hurried over to help her load all of the supplies she thought a kitten would need into her car.

James laughed. "It's just a little kitten," he remarked. He held the kitten up for Angelica to see.

Angelica laughed, too. "I know, but he will grow. We may as well be prepared."

James handed the kitten to Angelica and turned to leave. Mark had finished loading the supplies and taken his seat in the car. James turned back to Angelica. "Is Cindy going to be working tomorrow?" he inquired.

"No," said Angelica. "She has the next two days off."

"I see," replied James. "Thanks for taking the kitten. I'll see you later."

James entered the car and headed to the station to check out for the day.

Cindy was very disappointed to see James' image fade in the mirror. She sighed heavily. Then, she turned around and smiled.

"I know he was smiling at me as the image faded," she observed. "I just have to be patient. We will meet in person very soon. I am so looking forward to meeting my own true love."

The phone rang as Cindy lay the mirror down. Cindy reached for it. She was surprised to see Melanie's name pop up on the screen. "Hello, Melanie," she answered. "What can I do for you?"

"Hello, Cindy, I was just talking to Valerie. I told her about the mirror display you made for the gallery. She asked if you could use the last mirror to make a display for her to use in the museum she manages in Denton. I told her it was fine with me, but I would ask you about it."

"Sure, I don't see why not. We may as well cause a sensation in Denton as well as Rolling Fork." Cindy laughed. "I'll get started on it as soon as I get back to work. How was the honeymoon?"

"They had a fabulous time, according to Valerie. I am just glad to know my daughter is so happy. Speaking of happy, how is your mirror working out?"

"My mirror is working out just fine," said Cindy smiling. "It showed me my guy. He is a gorgeous hunk. I can't wait for us to get together."

"Do you know him?" asked Melanie.

"I know who he is, now. We just haven't met in person, yet, only in the mirror."

"He can see you, too?" asked Melanie.

"Sometimes, we have talked a couple of times. The mirror doesn't let us talk for long at a time. I think it is playing with us," said Cindy.

"I had no idea the mirror could do all of that!" exclaimed Melanie. "This is very exciting,"

"Yes, it is exciting," agreed Cindy.

"Well, you hang in there. If anyone deserves to find true love, it's you," said Melanie.

"Thanks, Melanie," said Cindy, touched. "I'll see you in a couple of days and work on Valerie's display."

After hanging up the phone, Cindy sat down with paper and pencil and started designing a display for Valerie. It would keep her mind off James for a little while, maybe.

# CHAPTER 8

*J*ames very much wanted to find Cindy and see how strong a connection they had. However, he did not have her phone number or address yet, and he had to be in court on the case of the boys in the park, so there was no time to look her up. He and Mark had been told to be there. Besides, he told the mayor he would talk to the Judge.

He got there early so he could catch the Judge in his chambers before court. When he arrived in the courtroom, Mark was already there. James told the bailiff he wanted to talk with the Judge before court. The bailiff told him to wait while he gave the message to the Judge.

James took a seat beside Mark to wait. He did not wait long before the bailiff was back.

"The Judge will talk to you and your partner now," he said.

James was surprised the Judge wanted to talk to Mark also, but he did not say anything. He and Mark rose and followed the bailiff back to the Judge's chambers.

The Judge was sitting at his desk going over the file about

the arrest. He looked up and smiled when James and Mark entered.

"Hello, Officer Michaels, I see you have been busy. How can I help you today?"

"I wanted to talk with you about the boys. I realize the case is not very strong, but I feel it is important to try and get through to these boys before they get into some serious trouble or join a gang," said James.

"I see," said the Judge. He smiled at James. "Do you have any suggestions for me?"

"I was thinking some community service might help them, but they should be assigned different projects. They will do better if they are not in a group. They feed each other's egos. They want to shine in their leader's eyes," James paused to see if the Judge had any comment.

"Yes, I see what you mean. I'll have to think on it," he said. The Judge turned to Mark. "You did a good job out there. Your quick thinking saved Officer Michaels from possible serious injury. I am glad to see the academy is turning out such able recruits."

"Thank you, Sir," said Mark.

The Judge turned back to James. "Thank you, Officer Michaels for bringing this matter to my attention. I will see you both in court," said the Judge.

James and Mark rose and followed the bailiff back to the courtroom. When they entered the courtroom, they saw that the mayor and David were there. The other boys were there with various family members. James nodded to the mayor and several of the fathers, as he and Mark took their seats to wait for court to start.

"All rise," said the bailiff. They all stood as the Judge entered and seated himself. "You may be seated," said the bailiff. He read the case number and called for the case to be heard.

The Judge waited while the boys all rose and faced him. "I have studied this case, and I want you boys to know you have been showing a lack of good judgment. You have been causing a lot of trouble. All of you need to know that attacks on our police officers will not be tolerated. You should be mentoring and helping, not bullying, the younger children.

So, I have decided to let you each learn a little about the law and how the police help our community and its people. Each of you boys will be assigned to a police officer for one month. You will ride along with them and watch their interactions with their job and community. I will receive a report on you each week.

I will talk to your teachers and get you excused from class, but you will be responsible for getting your homework assignments and turning them in. At the end of this assignment, I will expect a written report from each of you. Those reports will be read by you in front of your school class. Are there any questions?"

The Judge paused but no one said anything. "Court dismissed," said the Judge.

"All rise," said the bailiff, as the Judge left the courtroom.

The mayor came over to James and Mark. He was smiling. "Thanks, Officer Michaels," he said.

James shook his head. "Don't thank me. This is the Judge's idea. Hopefully it will work out." James and Mark nodded to everyone and left the courtroom.

"When do we find out which boy will be with us?" asked Mark.

"We will probably have one by tomorrow. I think we will probably end up with David," said James with a sigh. "I had no idea the Judge was going to come up with this plan."

"Why do you think we will end up with David?" asked Mark.

"Because, the mayor will talk to the chief and arrange it," he said.

Mark laughed. "Yeah, I can see him doing that."

# CHAPTER 9

Cindy did her laundry and finished rearranging her room and the kitchen. She was bored. She stayed around the house hoping to hear from James. She knew he was probably working, but she was so excited to think she would be seeing him sometime soon.

"I can't stand this another minute," said Cindy. She grabbed her keys, her purse, and her mirror. She decided to go to the gallery and pick up the things she would need to build a display for Valerie. She could work on it at home while she waited to hear from James.

She let herself in the back door of the gallery. Melanie was at the cash register and waved at Cindy when she saw her coming down the hall.

"You can't stay away," she teased.

"I thought I could take some things home with me and work on Valerie's display there, if it is alright with you," explained Cindy.

"It's fine, but are you sure you want to spend your time off working on the display?" she asked.

"I'm bored waiting for something to happen. I need to keep busy."

Melanie smiled. "Well, take whatever you want, but if something better comes along, go for it."

"I will," laughed Cindy.

The bell over the door rang and Melanie went back up front.

Cindy started gathering things to take with her. She lay her purse on the work table. She started to lay her mirror down with it, when something caught her attention. She could see James and Mark reflected in a large picture window in an abandoned store. They were across the street from the window. They were being attacked by three men. James was facing her with his back to the alley. He could not see another man sneaking up behind him. The man had a bat in his hand and was about to hit James with it.

"Look out," screamed Cindy.

James seemed to hear her. He started to turn, but it was too late. The man hit him on the head with the bat. James crumpled to the ground and was not moving. Mark continued to fight, but he was losing with four guys on him. He was taking a beating.

Cindy grabbed her phone and dialed 911. "Hello, what is your emergency?"

"You have an officer needing assistance at the abandoned stores on Camp Street. One officer is down and the other is outnumbered."

"Who is this?"

"My name is Cindy Lawson. Stop wasting time and get some help out there," Cindy demanded.

"The help is on its way, Miss Lawson,"

"What's going on?" asked Melanie. She had heard Cindy yell and hurried back.

Cindy was still watching James in the mirror. He was still lying there and, so far, he had not moved.

"James and Mark were just attacked," she said, she was afraid to take her eyes off of the mirror. She saw more police cars and an ambulance pull to a stop. The officers went to help Mark and the EMTs went to James. "Good, they have help." Cindy told Melanie. Melanie looked in the mirror, but she could not see anything but her and Cindy's reflection.

"The ambulance is loading James up. They will take him to the hospital. I have to get over there." She grabbed her purse and keys and her mirror and started for the door.

"Let us know how he is," requested Melanie.

"I will," promised Cindy with a wave as she left.

Cindy entered the hospital. She started walking toward the nurse's station, but she saw Alex coming down the hall toward her. "Alex," she called.

Alex looked up, startled to see Cindy looking so upset. "Cindy is anything wrong?" he asked. He stopped in front of her and waited for her to answer.

"The officers who were brought in by ambulance just now. Are they alright?" she asked.

"They are going to be just fine. Officer Black Feather is being treated for cuts and bruises. Officer Michaels has come around. He is a little groggy and has a concussion, but he will be fine. Why are you asking?"

"Can I see James for a few minutes? We are friends." She added, in answer to his question.

Alex studied her for a minute. "He is still in ICU." Cindy looked at him pleadingly. "Alright, come with me. I'll let you see him for a minute. No excitement, please. He has to stay calm." Cindy followed Alex down the hall. He stopped at a door and pushed it open. "Are you up for a visitor, James?" he asked.

James looked over and saw Cindy peeping around Alex. A big smile lit up his face. Then he winced and toned it down. "I most certainly am up for a visitor. Hello, Beautiful," he said.

Cindy entered the room and hurried to his side and grasped his hand. "I have been so worried about you," she said.

"You can only stay five minutes," said Alex as he left.

"When I saw you get hit, I was so afraid," said Cindy.

"You saw me get hit?" asked James.

"Yes, in the mirror. There was a reflection in the window. I called 911 and told them to send help." Cindy squeezed his hand. "I don't think I have ever been so scared."

"Thank you," said James. He drew her hand up kissed it. "You probably saved our lives. I am so glad we can finally talk face to face," said James.

"Me, too," agreed Cindy. She hugged his hand and rubbed her cheek against it.

James raised his hand up and cupped the side of her face. He gently pulled her face down and placed a gentle kiss on her lips.

Cindy savored the contact and sighed when he pulled back.

"So," said James with a grin. "True love?"

"Oh," said Cindy. "You saw the display at the gallery."

"Yeah," he agreed. "It was very enlightening. Is that the mirror you were looking in?"

"No," said Cindy. "I have my own. Melanie brought three back from Italy. I fixed a display for the gallery with one. I'm working on a display for a museum in Denton with the second mirror. Melanie gave me the third mirror. Would you like to see it?"

Cindy pulled the mirror out of her purse and handed it to James. He looked it over and handed it back to Cindy.

"It looks like a regular mirror to me," he said.

"Did I hear you say you saw James and Mark get attacked in the mirror?" asked a voice from the door.

James and Cindy looked around, startled. They had not noticed anyone standing there. "Come on in Marsha. This is Cindy. Cindy, this is Marsha Dane, she is from the police station. They send her out whenever an officer is injured."

"Hello, Mrs. Dane, Yes I saw James and Mark were in trouble and called 911 for help," she answered.

"May I see the mirror?" asked Marsha.

Cindy took the mirror to Marsha and let her hold it.

Marsha caught her breath on a gasp. She stared into the mirror like she couldn't believe her eyes. She turned white as a sheet.

"Brian," she whispered. "They told me you were dead. Where are you?" She couldn't take her eyes off of the mirror.

James and Cindy looked on astonished as Marsha looked into the mirror.

"Who do you see in the mirror?" asked Cindy.

"It is my husband, Brian. He has been missing for three years. He disappeared on a buying trip for the company he worked for. We found his car. It was completely burned. I was told he could not have survived. I looked for a year. I couldn't find any trace of him. I finally accepted that he was gone," she had tears in her eyes as she continued looking in the mirror.'

"Do you see anything to help you identify where he is?" asked James.

"Well, he is standing in front of a large mirror. He has a scar on the side of his face and I see a sign saying Danny's Bar and Grill. He looks like he is working there."

Brian looked up at the mirror and saw Marsha looking at him. He looked behind himself and then turned back to the mirror. Brian smiled at Marsha and then he looked puzzled. "Do I know you?" he asked.

"Yes, you know me, Brian. It's Marsha, your wife. Where are you?"

"My wife," he replied. "My name isn't Brian, my name is Wes. I am in Sharpville."

"Where is Sharpville," she asked.

"It's in Kansas." He replied.

Cindy and James listened in astonishment as Marsha carried on a conversation with the mirror.

Marsha suddenly lost the connection with the mirror. She looked at Cindy like she was about to cry. "Can you get it back?" she asked.

Cindy shook her head. "The mirror has a mind of its own. It will only show what it wants to, or what it thinks you need to see. There is no way to control it." Marsha handed the mirror to Cindy. Cindy shook her head. "You keep it for now. I have already found my true love. When you get Brian back, you can return it to the gallery. Good luck."

She leaned over and gave Marsha a hug. Marsha hugged her back. "Thanks, good luck to the two of you. You take care, James. Your partner is doing well. He has some cuts and bruises, but he will heal. He held his own in the fight. He made a good showing for himself. I'll see you later."

Marsha hurried out to start her search for her lost husband.

"It was nice of you to let her keep the mirror," remarked James.

Cindy smiled. She leaned forward and kissed James gently. "I don't need it anymore. It already brought us together. Its ready to help someone else."

James smiled and kissed her again. "I will look forward to getting out of here so we can get to know each other," He put his arm around her and held her close.

"They did not give me a beautiful girl to help me heal," said a voice from the door.

"Hi, Mark," said James. "You look a mess. Everyone has been saying you were okay. They need their eyes checked."

Cindy punched him gently on the arm. "Be nice, if he had not kept those guys busy until help came, they may have killed you both."

"You are right, Cindy. Thanks, Mark for using your face to keep them busy."

Mark laughed and then he groaned, "Please don't make me laugh. I'm headed home. I'll see you tomorrow."

They said "good night" to Mark, and Cindy looked back at James.

"I'm going to have to go, too. Alex said I could only stay five minutes. It has been at least thirty minutes."

"Before you go, I want your phone number and address. I would like to know how to find you when I get out of here."

Cindy saw his phone on the table beside the bed. She put her number in his phone. Then, she took out her phone and called her number with his phone so she would have his number. She searched in her purse for a piece of paper and a pen. She wrote her name and address on the paper. She lay the phone down and handed him the paper.

James looked at the paper and his eyes widened.

"You only live a couple of blocks from me. How did we miss meeting until now?" he asked.

"Moon Walking would say the universe knew when we should meet," said Cindy with a smile.

"Who am I to argue with Moon Walking?" James agreed.

"I'll see you tomorrow," said Cindy with a gentle kiss good night. She left reluctantly.

James relaxed with a sigh and a happy smile. Tomorrow was looking very nice. He closed his eyes to dream about reflections of true love.

# CHAPTER 10

*C*indy went by the gallery after leaving the hospital. In her hurry to get to James, she had forgotten the supplies to work on the display for Valerie. She also promised Melanie an update on James and Mark. She went to the front room, after entering through the back door.

"Hi," she greeted Melanie.

"Hello," said Melanie. "How is James?"

"He's doing okay. I managed to get to see him for a few minutes. Alex was nice enough to let me in. James has a concussion and has to stay overnight. Mark Black Feather is okay, too. He had a lot of cuts and bruises, but they released him and let him go home."

"Did they catch the guys?" asked Melanie.

Cindy looked startled. "You know, in all of the excitement, I forgot to even ask about them. With all of the police on the scene, I would think they would catch at least some of them. I guess I will find out tomorrow." Cindy paused before continuing.

"Something very interesting happened with my mirror while I was with James at the hospital. They sent Marsha

Dane, the police liaison officer, to the hospital to check on James and Mark. She heard James and me talking about the mirror. She wanted to see it, so, I showed it to her.

As soon as she looked in the mirror, she turned white as a sheet and called out the name Brian. It turns out, Brian is her husband. He was presumed dead three years ago. He was involved in a car accident. Marsha was told there was no way he could have survived. But, he did somehow. She talked to him in the mirror. I let Marsha keep the mirror until she can figure things out. She is going to return it here after she finds Brian."

"Wow!" said Melanie. "It sounds like you have had quite a day. It was nice of you to let her borrow the mirror."

"I had to," said Cindy. "I found my guy. The mirror has more people to help."

Melanie gave her a hug. "You are an amazing person, Cindy. I'm glad we are friends."

Cindy smiled mistily. "I'm glad, too," she said hugging Melanie back.

"I better gather up my supplies and head home," said Cindy. "I'll see you in a couple of days." Cindy pulled away and hurried to the back room to gather her supplies for Valerie's display. She wanted to hurry home and check on James.

As Cindy was entering her house, her phone rang. She dropped her keys in their bowl and rummaged in her purse for her phone. She lay her purse down and answered. "Hello," she said.

"Hello, Beautiful."

"James," she said, smiling. "How are you? Aren't you supposed to be resting?"

"How can I rest with the nurses checking every thirty minutes to see if I am alright?" he answered.

"Poor baby, you just keep your mind off those nurses. I saw how they fussed over you," she teased.

"You are the only one on my mind. I had to try out your number. I wanted to make sure you were real and I had not dreamed you."

"I'm very real," she replied. "I know our meeting was unusual, but we are meant to be together."

"I have been dreaming about you ever since I first saw you in the mirror," James assured her.

"I have been dreaming about you, too," said Cindy. "I am so glad I can touch and hold you for real."

"Me, too. I should be out of here tomorrow. I'll probably get a few days off. We can spend them together," said James.

"I would like that," agreed Cindy. "Melanie asked if they caught the guys who were attacking you and Mark. I forgot to ask about them before. All I could think about was you."

"I'm glad all you are thinking about is me," said James. "They are all under arrest. I don't think the Judge is going to go easy on them. They have the bat I was hit with and were able to get fingerprints off it."

"Good, I didn't want to have to explain about the mirror to the Judge. I don't think he would believe me," said Cindy seriously. "I hate to hang up, but you need to rest. Call me in the morning, and I'll pick you up when you are released." Cindy said.

"Thanks, Beautiful. I'll see you then," James said softly.

They each hung up their phones. Both had huge smiles on their faces and dreamy looks in their eyes.

Marsha Dane went straight to her office as soon as she returned to police headquarters. She turned on her computer and looked up Sharpville, Kansas. It was a small town. The closest airport would be in Kansas City. She printed out a route from the airport to Sharpville. She booked a flight to Kansas City for the next day. Next, she reserved a rental car. She looked up motels in Sharpville. The bed and breakfast looked like the best deal, so she reserved a room for a week. She did not know how long she would need it.

After she had all of the arrangements made, she went to the Chief's office and knocked on the door.

"Come in," called the Chief. He looked up and smiled at Marsha as she stood in front of his desk. "Have a seat, Marsha. What can I help you with?"

"I need to take the next month off. I have a family problem I have to deal with," Marsha stated quietly.

"Is there anything I can help with?" asked the Chief.

"No, only I can deal with it. I just need the time off," she stated firmly.

The Chief looked at her for a minute. He shrugged. "Okay, Marsha. You have your month. If you need more time or if there is anything any of us can do to help just let us know. You take care of yourself and keep in touch."

"Thank you, Chief. I will keep in touch," she replied.

Marsha quickly left his office. She went back to her office and gathered all of the information she found and put it in a folder. She put her airline and rental car confirmation in her purse. She looked around to see if she was forgetting anything. She shook her head, squared her shoulders, and left her office. She was going to find Brian.

When Marsha arrived home, she went to pack a suitcase. She carried her packed suitcase, her purse, and the folder and put them by the front door. After taking a shower and laying out traveling clothes, she set her alarm clock. She did not want to miss her plane.

Before she lay down, she took the mirror and gazed into it again. At first it showed only her reflection, but as she continued to look, the mirror changed. She found herself gazing into the mirror at Danny's Bar and Grill. Brian was sitting on a stool at the bar. He had his head leaning on his arms and looked to be deep in thought.

She studied him with tears in her eyes. She had missed him so much. Brian must have felt her looking at him. He lifted his head and looked into the mirror. He did not recognize her. He did not know who she was.

Marsha wiped away her tears. Brian was the love of her life. If he did not know her, she would make sure he was reacquainted with their love.

Brian could see the determination on her face.

"I'm coming, my love," said Marsha. The mirror faded out.

Marsha turned out the light and went to bed. She needed some sleep. Tomorrow was going to be a long day.

# CHAPTER 11

*W*hile Marsha was on a plane flying to Kansas, Cindy was on her way to the hospital to check on James. She was too impatient to wait for a phone call. He was already dressed and ready to leave when she arrived. He was standing beside his bed and looked up with a grin when she entered, after a short knock on the door.

Cindy walked straight into his arms. They opened and then closed around her. The two of them hugged and exchanged a quick kiss.

"You were supposed to call me," said Cindy. She was gazing lovingly into his eyes.

"Mark stopped by my place and picked up a change of clothes for me. I am waiting on my release papers. I wanted our next meeting to be with me on my own two feet," James hugged her close again.

There was a knock at the door, and the Chief of police opened the door and entered. James did not let go of Cindy, but he did release one hand so he could shake hands with the Chief.

"How are you doing, James?" he asked.

"I'm doing better. I am waiting to be released," answered James.

"I am glad to hear it," said the Chief. "I'm giving you and Officer Black Feather the rest of the week off."

"Thank you, Sir," answered James.

"No. Thank you for being such a good addition to our police department. Both, you and Officer Black Feather, have been put in for a commendation."

"We were just doing our job, Sir," James replied.

"You went above and beyond," He looked at Cindy snuggled close to James' side.

James glanced down at Cindy and smiled. "This is Cindy Lawson, Sir. Cindy, this is our chief of police, Captain Jacobs,"

The Chief held out his hand to Cindy.

"It is nice to meet you, Miss Lawson. How are things at the gallery?"

Cindy looked at him, surprised he knew she worked at the gallery. "Everything is fine at the gallery, Sir. It is nice to meet you."

The Chief smiled seeing her look of puzzlement. "I have been friends with the Masons for years. Your name has come up a few times. They are very fond of you. I also know you were the one to call for help for Officer Michaels and Officer Black Feather. Thank you."

"I was so afraid when I saw James fall," she said looking up at James lovingly. James smiled down at her.

The Chief turned his attention back to James.

"The Judge is pushing the hearing on your attackers through quickly. He wants to let the gangs know that this type of behavior will not be tolerated. So, your time off maybe interrupted to appear in court. You will be notified. I will see you next week." He shook James' hand, nodded goodbye to Cindy, and departed.

Shortly after the Chief left, Mark entered the room. "I have your release papers," he told James, waving the papers in the air. "Good morning, Miss Lawson."

"Good morning, Mark. Please call me Cindy," Cindy remarked.

"Thank you, Mark. You just missed the Chief," said James.

"I talked to him in the hallway. He filled me in about court and taking the rest of the week off," said Mark.

"Are you going to need a ride home?" asked Mark.

"No," said James. "Cindy will give me a lift. Thanks for bringing my clothes.

"Sure, if you need any help, just call," Mark gave a small wave and departed.

James gave Cindy another hug and pulled back. "Let's get out of here," he said. He grabbed his bag and papers and they started to walk down the hall toward the nurses' station.

They did not stop at the nurses' station, but continued onto the elevator. James nodded to the nurse on duty as they passed. Most of his attention was on Cindy. The elevator carried them down to the lobby. While on their way down, James gave Cindy a quick kiss and hug. Cindy hugged him back and gave him a big smile.

When the doors opened, there were some people waiting to board the elevator. They smiled at James and Cindy. It was obvious how they had occupied themselves during the ride. James and Cindy smiled at everyone and exited the elevator so the others could enter.

When in the car, they decided they would go to James' house first. Cindy wanted to see where he lived. If he felt up to it, they would go on to Cindy's house. Cindy did not care where they went. She just wanted to spend the time getting to know her guy.

They pulled into James' driveway and stopped. "Wow," said Cindy. "You really are close to me."

"Yeah," agreed James. "I cannot believe how close we were. We were meant to meet. I am glad the mirror hurried things along."

"Me, too," said Cindy.

They got out of the car and went to the door. James unlocked it and reached around to turn on the light before standing back and inviting Cindy in.

James looked around to see if he left any dirty clothes lying around. He gave a sigh of relief. Everything looked to be in fairly good shape.

Cindy smiled when she heard the sigh. "Relax," she said. "I know you were not expecting company. Anyway, I just want to be with you."

James pulled her close to him. "We are finally alone and I can do this," he said

He kissed her, deeply and satisfyingly. Cindy hugged him and kissed him back. They finally stopped so they could breathe. They still held each other tightly.

"Wow!" said Cindy.

"Yeah, wow!" agreed James. "I don't think I will ever get enough of you. You are in my heart and soul. We may just be starting out, but I want you to know, I am in this for the duration. You are my other half."

"I feel the same way," agreed Cindy. "I am so glad I did not settle for anyone else. I waited to find you. You are my other half, too."

This called for another long and satisfying kiss.

James smiled at Cindy. "Do you want to come into the living room? We haven't made it past the entrance."

"Sure," she replied. "Although," she added, "I am thoroughly enjoying the entrance."

James took her hand and led her into the living room. Cindy looked around. The room was quite cozy, considering it was decorated for a bachelor. There was a long brown plush sofa. It had tables at each end. The tables had lamps shaped like cars on them. The shades on the lamps had pictures of race cars on them.

"I have never seen any lamp's like these," she remarked.

"They were a housewarming gift from my sister," remarked James.

He was urging her toward the sofa, while giving her time to look around.

"I like them," said Cindy. She looked at the large television and the music system beside it. "Nice," she said with a smile.

James managed to get her to the sofa. He sat down and pulled her down beside him. Cindy immediately snuggled up into his arms. James gave her a quick kiss. When he pulled back, Cindy gave him a questioning look. "I'm not in this just for sex. Don't get me wrong, I love the sex, but I want to get to know more about what makes Cindy Lawson tick."

Cindy grinned at him. "Okay, we will talk. Then, can we get to the sex part?" she teased.

"Yeah, we sure can," agreed James, with a laugh.

"My name is Cindy Lawson. I'm twenty-eight years old. I have a mother and father and two brothers. They all still live on the family farm. It is about eighty miles from here. The closest town to them is Denton. We don't get together as much as we should, but I try to visit when I can around the holidays. Both of my brothers are married. The elder has two children, a boy and a girl.

I went to college here in Rolling Fork. Valerie was my

roommate. We became friends. Since I was majoring in graphic design, Valerie persuaded her parents to offer me a job at the gallery when I graduated. I have been working there for six years and I love it. Melanie and Frank treat me like family. There you have it. All about Cindy Lawson. Now, it is your turn. Tell me all about James Michaels."

"A good start, but I have a feeling I will be learning about Cindy Lawson for years to come," said James, with a smile.

"Oh, I hope so," replied Cindy, giving him a small kiss. "Now, tell me all about you."

"My name is James Michaels. I am thirty-four years old. My parents and my sister live about two hundred miles from here in the small town of Saxon. My father owns and runs the hardware store. My sister has a beauty parlor. Mom helps dad in the store. My sister married her high school sweetheart last year.

I did not want to work in a hardware store. I have always wanted to be a policeman. So, when I turned eighteen, I joined the police academy. I love the work. I love being out on the street. When one of the other cadets told me about an opening here, I applied and was accepted. The Chief has been good to me. I have been with the department twelve years. The Chief keeps pushing me to accept more rank, but I am afraid if I do it will put me in a desk job. I'm not ready for a desk. I want to be out there helping people and making a difference. So, there you have it. Are you ready to run for the hills?" asked James, smiling.

"No," replied Cindy. "I'm ready to hold on tightly and never let go."

James smothered her face with kisses, before zooming in for a long passionate kiss on the lips.

"We will both hold on tightly," whispered James.

"Yes," agreed Cindy.

There was no talking for a while. They were interrupted by the ringing of James' phone. James looked at the screen and saw the Chief's name pop up.

"Yes, Sir," he answered.

"The bailiff called to let me know the hearing on your attackers is scheduled for tomorrow at ten. I have already informed Officer Black Feather. Will you be able to make it?" he asked.

"I'll be there," promised James. "Thank you for letting me know."

"No problem," answered the Chief as he hung up.

Cindy looked at him inquiringly.

"The hearing on the attackers is set for ten in the morning," James pulled her close to him again. "Now, where were we?"

"I don't know," Cindy said teasingly. "Maybe we should start at the beginning, and go from there."

James started tickling her. Cindy squealed with delight. She tried to tickle him back, but she was laughing so hard she couldn't get a good hold.

She finally decided to play dirty. She unbuttoned the first three buttons on his shirt and started spreading kisses all over the open skin on his neck and chest.

James answered with a groan, but he was distracted from his tickling.

James' phone rang again. He didn't look at it as he gave a distracted hello.

"Hello, James," answered Mark.

"Hi, Mark. What's up?" he asked.

"Did the Chief call you about court in the morning?" asked Mark.

"Yes," answered James.

"I was wondering if you needed me to come by and pick you up?" asked Mark.

"Do you have the patrol car?" inquired James.

"No, one of the officers drove it to the station. I have my own car. I can pick you up in it."

James thought for a minute. Then, he turned to Cindy. "Do you think you could drive me to court in the morning? You might enjoy watching the proceedings," said James.

"I would like that," agreed Cindy,

"Mark," James said into the phone. "Cindy is going to drive me in. Thanks for asking."

"I heard," laughed Mark. "Have a good night."

"You, too," said James as he hung up the phone.

"Would you like to go out and get some food?" asked James. "We could go by your house and pick up something for you to wear in court."

"Oh, so I'm staying here tonight?" she inquired, with a raised eyebrow.

"I hope so," said James seriously.

Cindy smiled. "I would love to go out to eat, and I absolutely have to get something to wear to court."

James grinned. He took her hand and pulled them both up from the sofa. "What type of food do you want?"

Cindy smiled. "I'm in the mood for Italian, in honor of a certain mirror."

"Italian it is," agreed James.

# CHAPTER 12

*T*he next morning, Cindy showered first and then went to the kitchen to start the coffee while James showered. She looked in the refrigerator to see if James had anything edible. She sighed. There was not much food. She was going to have to do a grocery run, later.

She found some bagels and put them in to toast. Then, she found some cream cheese and laid it out. She heard James coming as the coffee finished. She looked in the cabinet and pulled down two cups, filling them both up before looking around for sugar and creamer.

"Good morning, Beautiful," said James coming up behind her and putting his arms around her. He started nuzzling her neck.

"Good morning," said Cindy. She turned in his arms and raised her lips for a good morning kiss. James happily obliged her. After a very satisfying kiss, Cindy motioned to the coffee. "Do you have any sugar and creamer?" she asked.

James reached over and pulled out the sugar bowl and the creamer from the cupboard. He pulled Cindy close again and gave her another kiss. James pulled back. "I know we have to get ready for court. I just want to feel you in my arms."

"I feel the same way," agreed Cindy. "We have the rest of the day after court."

They each ate a bagel, spread with cream cheese, and drank their coffee. When they went out to the car, Cindy handed James the keys. She could tell he had an aversion to being driven. James grinned at her as he took the keys.

When they pulled into the parking lot at the court house, Mark was getting out of his car. They all went inside together. They had just sat down when the bailiff came and told them the Judge wanted to see them in his chambers. He said the Judge wanted to see Cindy, also.

Cindy was surprised, but she arose and, holding tightly to James' hand, followed the bailiff, along with James and Mark, to the Judge's chambers.

The bailiff knocked on the Judge's door and received a "Come in."

"Here are the officers and Miss Lawson, as you requested, your Honor."

"Thank you," said the Judge. "Thank you all for coming. James, are you recovering from your injuries?" he asked.

"I'm doing fine, Your Honor," replied James.

The Judge turned to Mark. He grimaced at the evidence of the attack, still visible on Mark's face. "How about you, Officer Black Feather?" the Judge inquired.

"It looks worse than it is. I'm getting better," replied Mark.

"Good," said the Judge. "The prisoners have all pled guilty, so there will not be a jury trial. The only thing left is sentencing. Miss Lawson, I understand you called for help."

"Yes, Your Honor," replied Cindy.

"Did you see the attack?" asked the Judge.

"Yes, in a way," replied Cindy.

"What do you mean?" asked the Judge puzzled.

"I saw the reflection of the attack in the window across from where they were attacked." answered Cindy.

"Where were you at the time?" asked the Judge.

"I was in the gallery, where I work."

"If you were in the gallery, how did you see the attack?" asked the Judge.

"I know this is going to sound impossible," said Cindy, she paused and drew a breath before she continued. "I saw the attack in my magic mirror."

The Judge studied her for a minute, and then he grinned widely. "I believe you, Miss Lawson," he said.

"You do?" asked Cindy.

"Yes, I do," he replied. "You see, I have had some experience with the magic mirror." As all four of them, including the bailiff, looked on in surprise, the Judge leaned back in his chair and grinned. "You see. Thirty years ago, I was just fresh out of law school and a group of us decided on vacation to Italy. One of the boys had a family villa there where we could stay. One day, I was standing gazing into a fountain when my reflection faded, and I was looking at a lovely young woman.

I looked around, but didn't see anyone. Then, there was a commotion across the viale. The woman I saw dashed out of the antique store and looked around wildly. She spotted me standing by the fountain and headed straight for me. When she reached me, I opened my arms, and she threw herself into them. She explained that I was her true love shown to her in a magic mirror. We went back to the store and tried to buy the mirror, but the man said it wasn't for sale. He had bought it for his daughter. We were married three weeks later and have been happily married for thirty years.

Of course, my wife told our daughter about the mirror and how we met. Now, my twenty-year-old daughter heard about the magic mirror at the gallery and goes there every day trying to see her true love. So, you see, Miss Lawson, I do believe you."

They had all sat and listened to the Judge in astonishment. James grinned when he thought about how his first sight of Cindy had been when he was shaving.

"I told the girls to be patient with the mirror. Their guys have to be somewhere with a reflective surface for the mirror to show them," said Cindy.

"Is the mirror in the gallery where you saw the attack?" asked the Judge.

"No," said Cindy. "I have my own mirror."

"Do you have it with you?" asked the Judge,

"No, I loaned it to Marsha Dane," said Cindy.

"Marsha, why Marsha?" asked the Judge.

"Marsha wanted to see it at the hospital. When she looked in the mirror, she called out her husband's name and turned white as a sheet. She talked to Brian and found out he was still alive. So, I loaned her the mirror until she could check it out."

"Brian is alive?" whispered the Judge.

"Yes," answered Cindy. "Do you know him?" asked Cindy.

"He is my Godson," answered the Judge. "If you hear anything from Marsha, will you let me know?"

"Yes, of course," answered Cindy.

The Judge pulled himself together. "Thank you all for coming in. I had better get ready for court," he said dismissing them. The bailiff showed them back to their seats.

"All rise. Court is in session," said the bailiff.

They all stood and waited for the Judge to enter and be seated.

"You may be seated," said the bailiff.

"Let the record show that all of the four defendants have pled guilty," said the Judge. "I will handle each case separately. The first case is Bobby Doss. Rise and face the court." He waited for the young man to stand, before he continued speaking. "Mr. Doss, you are accused of assaulting a police officer with a bat. Do you stand by your guilty plea?"

"Yes, Your Honor,"

"I sentence you to twenty years. Five years will be suspended, and you will have five years of probation. If you get into any trouble, the additional ten years will be added back to your sentence. Bailiff, take the prisoner out."

He waited until the prisoner was taken out before going on to the next case. "The next case is Stanley Martin. Please rise and face the court." Stanley Martin rose and faced the Judge. "Mr. Martin do you stand by your guilty plea?" asked the Judge.

"Yes," said Stanley.

The Judge stared at Stanley for a minute. He finally gave a sigh and continued. "Mr. Martin, this is the fifth time you have appeared before me. You have been warned, repeatedly, to straighten up. You have ignored the warnings and worn out my patience. You are a very bad influence on the young people in this community. I have no choice but to sentence you to time. Mr. Martin you are sentenced to fifteen years. With good behavior you can be released in ten. Bailiff, remove the prisoner."

The Judge waited for Stanley to be removed before turning the final two prisoners. "Bastion Belk and Sammy Storm please rise and face the court. You have both pleaded guilty. Do you each still stand by your plea?" The Judge inquired.

"Yes, Your Honor," both boys responded.

"I have looked into your records. You are both nineteen. You are both high school dropouts. You made good grades when you were in school. I have a choice for you to make. You can take ten years in prison, or you can take a term in the marines. I have someone waiting to give you your GED test, and I have a recruiter waiting to sign you up after you pass. So, which will it be boys? The choice is yours."

The Judge did not have to wait long before both boys picked the Marines.

"Bailiff, take Mr. Belk and Mr. Storm into conference room C. Stay with them until they finish the tests and fill out the recruiter's papers. Then turn them over to the recruiter."

"All rise," said the bailiff.

The Judge left the courtroom, and the bailiff took the two boys out.

James, Cindy, and Mark rose and left the courtroom. "He doesn't mess around," commented Cindy.

"He is strict, but he is fair. It hard to help some people," remarked James.

"They are lucky they were not on the reservation. They do not mess around when it comes to breaking the rules," remarked Mark. "Well, I will see you the day after tomorrow. We will start our first day with our young ride-along."

James just shook his head. "Yeah," he agreed. "See you then."

James and Cindy went toward her car. "What did he mean about a young ride-along?" she asked

"It's some young boys we busted for bullying. The Judge is making them ride along with a police officer for a month. He thinks it might make them stop and think."

Cindy laughed. "If anyone can help them its you," she said.

James pulled her close and kissed her gently. "If we weren't in public, I could do better," he said.

"Well, why are we still in public?" asked Cindy.

They hurried into the car and headed for home.

# CHAPTER 13

hen Marsha landed at the Kansas City airport, she collected her suitcase and followed the signs to the car rental. After she filled out the necessary papers, she took possession of the car. She sat in the car for a few minutes and studied the directions to the small town of Sharpville. "Well, here I go," said Marsha.

She left the airport and entered traffic. She was on her way to find Brian! After driving about a hundred miles, Marsha pulled into a small gas station attached to a small store full of snacks and drinks. Marsha used the restroom and stocked up on snacks and some soft drinks. She added a few bottles of water and decided to fill her tank with gas, while she was there. She was hoping not to make another stop, before reaching her destination.

She drove into the town of Sharpville early in the afternoon. Marsha drove to the bed and breakfast and checked in. After she received her room key, Marsha asked for directions to Danny's Bar and Grill. When she asked, the desk clerk looked at her in a funny way, but he gave her the requested directions. She dumped her suitcase in her room and headed out to find Brian.

It was easy to find a place to park in the large parking area. There were not a lot of cars there. It was still early for the evening crowd to show up. Marsha entered the door and stopped. She looked around the room. Everyone in the room stopped talking and stared at her. She did not see Brian anywhere. She walked over to the counter and sat on a stool. The swinging door to the back room, opened, and Brian entered.

Brian stopped abruptly, when he saw Marsha sitting at the bar. Someone entering behind him bumped him and told him to move out of the way. Brian moved over, but he continued to stare at Marsha. He slowly walked over to the bar and stood in front of her. "You're the lady in the mirror," said Brian.

"Yes," Marsha nodded. Her heart was beating wildly. "You are my husband, Brian."

"I told you, my name is Wes," he replied.

Marsha shook her head. "You are Brian," she repeated. Marsha reached into her purse and withdrew her wallet. She opened it to her pictures and found one of her and Brian. They were laughing and gazing into each other's eyes. She showed the picture to her husband.

Brian took the wallet and looked at the picture. He was visibly shaken. "He looks like me, but he's missing one thing," he said.

"What is that?" asked Marsha. Brian pointed to the scar down the right side of his face. "Three years ago," she explained, "my husband Brian went on a buying trip for the company he worked for. He was in a very bad accident. His car was smashed and caught on fire. There was nothing left of it, but ashes. Everyone told me there was no way anyone could have survived the crash and fire." Marsha looked into his eyes. "You did survive. I don't know how, but you are Brian and you are alive. If you were not Brian, the mirror would not have shown you to me."

"What mirror?" Brian asked.

Marsha took the mirror out of her purse and showed it to Brian. "This is a magic mirror. When a woman looks into it, she will see her true love. You are my true love Brian. You always have been."

Brian took the mirror from her and looked it over. He frowned and handed it back to her. "It just looks like a mirror to me," He shrugged. Marsha was beginning to look frustrated. Brian looked at her for a minute, then, he sighed. His face softened. "Alright," he said "I did get this scar three years ago. I don't remember what happened. I did not even know who I was. A truck driver picked me up on the side of the road. My face was bloody and my clothes were a mess. He wanted to take me to a clinic, but I told him not to and proceeded to fall asleep. He said he tried to wake me a couple of times, but both times, I just mumbled something and went back to sleep. The truck driver let me ride to this town. This was the end of the line for him, so he woke me and told me this was as far as he was going. I got out and looked around. I saw a sign saying Westlake Trucking. So, I became Wes. Danny's Bar and Grill was across the road from me. So, I came in to see if I could get something to eat. I didn't have a wallet. All the money I had was a twenty in my pocket." The words flooded out. His face was lost in memory. After a moment, he continued.

"Danny fixed me a plate. While I was eating, we got to talking. Danny offered me the room around back and a job working here. I took both, gratefully." Brian came around the bar to face Marsha. He stood in front of her and gazed into her eyes. "I knew we were connected as soon as I saw you in the mirror." Brian admitted. He put his hand, gently on her soft and perfect face. "Are you sure you want to live with this scared face?" he asked.

"Oh, Brian, I love you, not just your face. I love the man inside. I love the man who held and comforted me when my mother died. I love the man who would rub my feet for me when I came home aching. I love the man who would cook for me, or order food when we were both too tired to cook. I love the man who I could snuggle up to and feel safe. I love the man who held me and cried with me when we lost our baby."

"We had a baby?" Brian interrupted.

"I had a miscarriage," said Marsha, "We never even got to hold him." Marsha sniffed back tears just thinking about it.

Brian pulled her close and hugged her. "I don't remember all of those things," he replied.

"Did you ever go to a doctor?" asked Marsha.

"Yeah, He told me I might get my memory back anytime. All it would take is the right stimulus."

While the two of them had been talking, everyone in the Bar and Grill had been fascinated observers. One of the waitresses eased up to Marsha. "Do you really have a magic mirror?" she asked.

"Yes," replied Marsha. "I don't know how it works. I only know it worked for me."

She took the mirror out of her purse and held it so the waitress could look in it. The waitress looked, but she only saw her own reflection. She sighed with disappointment.

When the other girls saw the waitress look in the mirror, they hurried over to get a chance to look. Marsha patiently stood and held the mirror so each girl could look. One of the girls gasped as she looked in the mirror. "Mason," she murmured.

Brian waited by Marsha's side until all of the girls had a chance to look. Marsha took Brian's hand. "I have a room rented. We can go there and talk some more."

"Okay," agreed Brian. "I'm taking the night off, Danny," he called.

Danny gave him a big smile and waved him on. He and Marsha went out to her car, and she drove them to her bed and breakfast. When they were in Marsha's room, she lay her purse on the dresser and turned to Brian. They stared into each other's eyes. Then, Marsha went into Brian's arms. They closed around her. She squeezed him, tightly.

"When they told me you were dead, a part of me died. I felt as if the best part of me was gone. I couldn't function. The Chief took me off patrol and gave me a desk job. He was afraid I would get hurt on the street. I barely existed the last three years. Then, I looked in the mirror, and there you were. I felt hope for the first time in three years. I felt myself coming alive. I had to get to you as fast as I could," Marsha whispered to Brian."

"I'm sorry," said Brian.

"It's not your fault," said Marsha. "I just wanted you to know we are a package deal. There is no way I am losing you again. I couldn't take it." Marsha leaned in and pressed her lips to Brian's. Brian held her closer and kissed her back. They lost themselves to the sensations and feelings of once again holding each other. When they, finally, had to come up for air, Marsha lay her head on Brian's chest, and he rested his chin on top of her head. They stood holding each other, while their breathing slowed.

"I don't have memories, but I know you were meant to be in my arms. I have felt drawn to you from the moment I saw you in the mirror. You called to me. I knew you were important to me," Brian told Marsha.

There was no more talking. Brian pulled Marsha close to him and proceeded to show her how she made him feel. Marsha cooperated fully. Marsha awoke slowly, the next morning. She opened her eyes and smiled at the sight of Brian, asleep beside her, holding her snugly in his arms. Brian stirred and opened his eyes. He looked at Marsha and smiled.

"Hello, Love," he whispered.

Marsha froze. "You used to say that to me every time I woke in your arms," said Marsha. She kept staring at Brian. Brian was staring back at her.

Brian froze too and looked like he was in shock. "I remember," he whispered. Brian's arms tightened around her. "I guess, a night in my wife's arms was all the stimulus I needed to remember," he said.

"You really remember everything?" asked Marsha.

"I remember us. I remember the wreck. I remember crawling away from the wreck. I remember it all," Brian sighed deeply. "It wasn't an accident," said Brian.

"What?" exclaimed Marsha, sitting upright in bed.

Brian pulled her back down into his arms. "I was sideswiped by a car of teenagers. They were drunk and showing off. They took off, fast, when they saw what they had done. My car rolled down the hill. The windshield broke out. I got this scar from the glass. When the car landed, it was upside down. All of the windows were out. I managed to get my seat belt unbuckled and crawled. I could smell the gas, so I was in a hurry to get as far as I could from the car. The explosion knocked me out, temporarily. I didn't have my wallet. It was lying on the passenger seat. I took it out to pay a toll and hadn't put it back in my pocket. When I came to, I started walking. The truck driver picked me up."

Marsha hugged Brian, tightly. "Are you going to report the boys?" she asked.

"No," answered Brian. "Hopefully, they learned something that night. Putting them in jail will not help them or their families. I want to forget about the accident and enjoy my life with you."

He proceeded to enjoy waking up with his wife in his arms. Marsha was with him all the way. She had three, lonely, years to make up for. She was not wasting another moment.

Later, the two of them strolled into Danny's Bar and Grill together. They both wore huge smiles.

"Well, well, look who is back," greeted Danny.

Brian went over to the bar and greeted Danny with a hand shake. "Hi, Danny, my name is Brian Dane and this is my wife Marsha. I have my memory back."

"It's nice to meet you, Mrs. Dane," said Danny.

"Please call me Marsha," said Marsha offering Danny a handshake.

"I'm glad you folks reconnected. The mirror you have must be really something," said Danny.

"Yes, I borrowed it from a friend. She found her true love with the help of the mirror and wanted to help me," explained Marsha.

"What happens now? Are you folks leaving?" asked Danny.

"We haven't talked about it, yet," said Brian. "I am just so glad to have my wife back. I can't think of anything else."

"I don't care where we live as long as we are together," declared Marsha.

"What about your job?" asked Brian.

"There are police departments everywhere. I'm sure I will have no trouble finding a job. When I was moved off the street and given the police liaison job, I received a promotion. I am a sergeant now," said Marsha, smiling at Brian.

"Wow, congratulations," said Brian, giving her a hug.

"We will talk later," said Marsha.

A group of girls had entered. They looked around until they spotted Marsha, and then they headed straight for her. Marsha smiled at Brian. She knew what the girls wanted. "Why don't you talk to Danny while I help these girls?" she said.

"Okay," agreed Brian, easing behind the counter.

Marsha took the mirror out of her purse and led the girls to a table, so they could sit and look in the mirror. After all of the girls had a look, Marsha joined Danny and Brian at the bar.

Brian put his arm around her and pulled her close to him. He could not stand to be this close and not touch. Marsha smiled up at him. "You were very patient with them," he said.

Marsha shrugged. "They want what we all want, to find true love. If Cindy had not let me look in the mirror, I would not have known you were here."

"I will have to thank her," Brian agreed.

"We have to let the Judge know you are alive. He was very upset when they told us you were gone." Marsha squeezed Brian's hand.

"I know. We will. I want to have you to myself for a bit, before life intrudes," Brian whispered in her ear.

Marsha put her arms around him and hugged him tightly. "I completely agree," she whispered.

"Come on, let's sit at a table, so we can talk." Brian led her over to a table and seated her. They sat and held hands. They stared into each other's eyes and said nothing.

"What do you want to talk about?" asked Marsha.

Brian started, and then seemed to collect himself. "I want to talk about where we are going to live," he said.

Marsha nodded. "You don't want to go back to Rolling Fork."

Brian shook his head. "I have got to know the people around here. They are good people. They have all been very kind to me. Danny gave me a job and a place to live when he did not even know me. He did all he could to help me. I owe him a lot. He wouldn't think so, because we became friends, and he made me a manager in the bar and grill. I like working here." He paused to think what else he could say.

Marsha took his hand and squeezed it. "It's alright. I understand. I told you, I can work anywhere. Rolling Fork lost its appeal for me while I have been alone the last three years. We can sell our house and find one here. It will take a little time to arrange everything, but it can be done. We have a healthy bank account, even after I return your life insurance money."

"I hadn't thought about the insurance money," said Brian.

"It is alright," said Marsha. "I did not spend any of it. I wanted you, not insurance money."

Brian leaned forward and kissed her. "Are you sure about this?" he asked.

"Yes, I want you to be happy. If you are happy, I will be happy."

"I love you," he whispered.

"I love you, too," said Marsha.

They looked around, and noticed everyone was smiling at them indulgently. Brian pulled her to her feet. "Danny told me to take as much time off as I needed. Let's drive around and let you see the town, before you decide to move here." Brian guided her outside, after a wave to Danny and the others in the bar and grill.

Marsha went along, but she had already made up her mind. Brian was here, so here was where she was going to be.

# CHAPTER 14

*I*n Rolling Fork, Cindy was back at work, and James and Mark were starting their first day back with David as their ride-along. The day was going along fairly quietly. They drove their regular patrol, but it seemed as if everyone was on their best behavior. They were making their regular pass through the park, when James pulled the patrol car over and stopped.

There was a small child sitting on the ground, crying her as if her heart was broken. There were some ladies across the way, but they were gossiping and paying no attention to the child.

James got out of the car and walked towards the child. Mark and David got out, also, but they just stood and watched James. James knelt down and spoke gently to the child. "What's the matter, princess? Why are you crying?"

The child stopped crying and looked up at James. When she saw who was there, she smiled and threw herself into James' arms. "Opicer J," she squealed.

"Why were you crying, Princess," asked James.

"Scruffy is lost, I can't find him," she said.

"Where was the last place you saw him?" asked James.

The little girl screwed her nose up and thought hard. "By the swide," she said, pointing at the slide. James, with the little girl in his arms, and Mark and David following, led the way to the slide. They all started looking around. James spotted a pink cotton leg sticking out from behind one of the slides. He gently set the little girl on the ground, retrieved Scruffy, and handed her to the little girl.

He walked over to the gossiping ladies. They turned, all smiles until they saw his face. "Nadine, why aren't you watching your children, especially Penny?" he asked.

"Sadie and Jill were keeping an eye on her," said Nadine.

"They are not old enough to keep an eye on her. It's your job to keep her safe. I found her sitting over by the road, crying. She could have been kidnapped and gone and you would not even have noticed. I have told you before, if you have to gossip, at least turn and face your children, so you will know what is happening to them. This is your last warning. If I find it happening again, I will report you. Do you understand?" James, paused, waiting for her answer.

"Yes, Officer Michaels. I understand," said Nadine.

James turned as Penny ran up and hugged him around the legs. James leaned down and picked her up. Penny kissed him on his cheek. "Thank you for finding Scruffy for me, Opicer J." She said.

"You are very welcome, Princess. You be a good girl and run and play," said James. Penny was off running as soon as James put her on the ground.

James gave the ladies a stern look and turned back toward the patrol car. Mark and David were following. They did not say anything, but David looked thoughtful.

They drove into the town area. Mark spotted Moon Walking. She had her arms loaded and was headed down the street. "There's Moon Walking. Could we stop and see if she needs any help?" he asked.

James pulled into the curb and stopped. They all got out and went up to Moon Walking. "Hello, Moon Walking," said James.

"Officer Michaels," she greeted him with a nod. "Thank you for helping Bobby and his Dad. He is a very special young man."

"It was my pleasure," said James. "Is there anything we can help you with?"

"I am on my way to the gallery. I am getting a ride home with Little Flower. You know her as Angelica Black," she said, when she noticed his puzzled expression. She turned and faced Mark. "You are doing very well, Officer Black Feather. You have a good teacher." She noticed his fading bruises and cuts. "Sometimes life is a hard teacher. You have learned well." Mark gave her a sheepish grin.

Moon Walking looked at David. She studied him for minute. "Make sure you are very well behaved when you meet the Governor. It is very important to your future. Pay attention to Officer Michaels, young David, he will always show you the correct road to follow. Thanks for stopping, Officer Michaels. I will see you at my grandson's wedding." Moon Walking gave another nod and continued on toward the gallery.

After she left, the three of them returned to the patrol car. "How did she know my name, and what did she mean about the Governor?" asked David.

"Moon Walking always knows," replied Mark. "You would do well to listen to her."

David sat back in his seat, deep in thought. James and Mark looked at each other and grinned.

James parked at the station and they went in to check out

for the day. They met Eric, as they entered. Eric put a hand on James' arm to stop him and pulled him to the side. "I want to thank you for helping out with Penny. I have tried to tell Nadine to watch the girls. She doesn't listen. It makes me sick, when I think what could have happened to Penny," Eric said.

James looked at Eric with compassion. "Penny's fine. I should have known, Nadine would call and complain," he said. "I told her, if it happened again, I would report her. Maybe, she will listen. I don't want anything to happen to my Goddaughter. I love that youngster."

"I know you do," agreed Eric. "She loves you, too. If you see Nadine not watching them again, let me know. I will get Nadine's Mom to move in with us to keep an eye on the girls. Nadine won't like it, but the girl's safety has to come first."

"Alright, I'll do that," agreed James. He and Eric shook hands, and after another thank you from Eric, he continued on to check out.

Mark and David had moved on into the station, but they were still close enough to hear James and Eric talking. David looked at James with curiosity. He was learning a lot about people and life with these officers.

The mayor came into the police station to pick up David. He came over and shook hands with James and Mark. "Are you ready to go, David?" he asked.

"Sure," agreed David. "I'll see you tomorrow, Officer Michaels and Officer Black Feather."

"See you then, David," agreed James and Mark.

Mark left in his car. James decided to go by the gallery to see if Cindy wanted him to pick up a take out, or if she wanted to go out to eat. He parked and went inside to be greeted by Melanie. Melanie seemed to be having a good time watching the girls gazing in the mirror. When one of the girls said she saw someone in the mirror, Melanie got a big smile on her face.

Melanie turned and saw James watching her. "Hello, Officer Michaels. Love makes the world go round," she said.

"I wouldn't disagree with that," he agreed. "Call me James. Officer Michaels is a mouthful."

"Okay, If you call me Melanie," agreed Melanie with a smile.

James agreed with a smile. "Is Cindy in the back?" he asked.

"Yes, she is. Go on back," she waved him toward the stockroom.

Cindy was at her desk making entries in her log book, when James entered. She looked up and broke into a huge smile. She got up and came to meet him.

James opened his arms to receive her. After a very satisfying kiss, James leaned back, slightly. "I was off duty and I thought I would see if you wanted me to pick up take out, or go out to eat, and I just could not stand another minute without touching you," whispered James.

Cindy smiled. "I know what you mean. I have been having withdrawal symptoms myself. Cindy leaned in for another kiss. James was happy to oblige her.

After the kiss, they stood close to each other. Cindy leaned back slightly. "I received a call from Marsha, today. She found Brian."

"He really is alive?" exclaimed James.

"Yes, and he has his memory back. She and Brian have already called the Judge. They are going to be in town next week. She has to talk to the Chief and take care of their house and her car. They are not planning on staying. She asked us not to say anything at the station until she gets a chance to talk to the Chief. Brian likes where he has been living and Marsha wants him to be happy. She is so glad to have found him alive; she has no problem moving there."

"I won't say anything," sighed James. "I am so happy for them. I can't imagine the pain she went through, when they told her Brian was dead." They held each other a little closer, thinking about what Marsha went through.

"Enough," said James. "She found him, thanks to his reflection in your mirror. This is a happy time."

'Yes," agreed Cindy, with a smile. "What are you in the mood for tonight?"

"You, just, you," said James.

"I meant for food," laughed Cindy. "I'm dessert."

"Hmmmm, I always did have a sweet tooth," he said smiling.

Cindy gave him another hug. "I'll be home in about thirty minutes. I'm almost done here." James gave her another quick kiss and left to pick up some food. Cindy sighed. Life could not be any better. Thank God for reflections. They certainly made life interesting.

Cindy quickly finished her book work, retrieved her purse and went to tell Melanie good night. Angelica had left earlier. Moon Walking came by and Angelica left early to take her home. Cindy did not get a chance to talk to Moon Walking, while she was there, but she noticed her watching the girls at the mirror. Moon Walking had a look of satisfaction on her face as she watched the girls staring in the mirror's reflection.

"Bye, Melanie, see you tomorrow," she called.

"Good night, Cindy. Have a good night."

As she was leaving, Cindy heard her tell the girls about Cindy meeting James because of the magic mirror. Cindy laughed. There would be even more girls coming in, when her story circulated.

# CHAPTER 15

*C*indy lay back in James' arms. They were stretched out on the sofa, supposedly watching television, but the television was mostly just noise in the background. Neither of them was paying any attention to it.

"Moon walking is expecting us at Angelica and Alex's wedding on Saturday," said Cindy.

"I know. She mentioned it when I saw her today," said James.

"Where did you see Moon Walking?" asked Cindy.

"She was walking down toward the gallery, and I stopped to see if she needed help," replied James.

"Oh," said Cindy, grinning. "I bet that was interesting."

"Yeah, she really spooked David. She told him to be on his best behavior when he meets the Governor."

"Is David planning a visit with the Governor?" asked Cindy.

"No, that's what spooked him," replied James.

Cindy laughed. "I think Moon Walking enjoys keeping everyone off balance. She had a look of satisfaction on her face, when she watched the girls looking in the mirror at the gallery."

"Speaking of the mirror, what are you going to do with it when Marsha brings it back?" asked James.

"I've been thinking about it. When I talked to Marsha, she told me how the girls are hurrying into Danny's Bar and Grill to get a look before she takes the mirror away. I have to talk to Melanie about it, but I was thinking I could make her up a display for Danny's. I don't need it any more, I have my true love." She stopped for a very satisfying kiss. "I think the mirror is made to be passed on."

"Whatever you want is fine with me. You are going to marry me, aren't you?"

Cindy looked at him with a smile. "I might, when you ask me," she replied.

James sat up and pulled Cindy up, facing him.

"Cindy Lawson, will you do me the honor of being my wife?" he said.

Cindy threw her arms around his neck in a tight hold. "Oh, yes, James Michaels, I certainly will," she whispered.

"Soon," whispered James.

"Soon," agreed Cindy.

When Cindy told Melanie her idea about the mirror, she was all for it. The more people the mirrors helped the better she liked it. Cindy finished up the display for Valerie's mirror and took it out to show Melanie. It was a little different from the mirror in the gallery, but Melanie loved it. She was sure Valerie would love it.

Since the mirror was bronze, Cindy had fashioned a

background of yellow. She made it to resemble a tree. The mirror was made to look like part of the tree. The sign under it said, "THE TREE OF LIFE INCLUDES LOVE." Under this it said, "Look in the mirror, some will find their true love."

"It is absolutely perfect!" exclaimed Melanie. "Thank you, Cindy.

"You are welcome. I had fun designing it."

Cindy admired the display while she took it back to the store room to stay until Valerie came for it. She sat at her desk and thought about how best to display the last mirror.

When James went to the station to start his day, he was met by Eric. Eric pulled him aside to talk.

"I decided not to wait for another incident. Last night I called Nadine's mom and talked to her about what was going on and how I was worried about the girls. She agreed to move in. We decided to tell Nadine her mom has been having a hard time making ends meet since the death of Nadine's dad, and I want to help her out. When I told Nadine about it, she was fine. I just couldn't sit around wondering when something was going to happen to one of my girls. I had to take action. Nadine's mom will be here by this weekend. Hopefully, everything will be okay until then."

James listened to him and nodded several times, while Eric was talking. "I'm glad she is coming. It will be a relief to know she will be there. The girls will love having her around," said James.

"Well, I just wanted to give you a heads up, in case you run into Nadine and the girls. We had better get to work. I will talk to you later," said Eric.

"Later," agreed James.

James spotted Mark and David waiting for him, but as he started toward them, the Chief came to his door and motioned for him to come into his office. James followed the Chief into the room.

"Have a seat, James," said the Chief,

James took the chair in front of the desk, and waited for the Chief to speak. The Chief looked off into space, thoughtfully, for a minute, and then he looked back at James.

"First, the commendations for you and Mark are due to be delivered next Tuesday at a press conference out front. Next, over the last several years, you have been offered advancements in rank. You did not want them because you did not want to work in the office. Well, you have the rank anyway."

The Chief opened a drawer and took out several papers.

"I just put your papers up until you decided to accept them. Along with your commendation, you will be getting the rank of Captain. I hope you can accept it gracefully. I'm going to be retiring next year and I want to put you up for the office when I do. Please keep it quiet, for now. I haven't told anyone, yet." The Chief paused to give James a chance to speak.

James sat there in shock. He had not been expecting anything like this. "I won't say anything, Sir. I don't know about the job. I have no experience at being in charge," said James.

"You have plenty of time to think about it, and I will train you when the time comes. I just wanted to give you a heads up about everything, so you wouldn't be blindsided."

The Chief rose, a signal to end the conversation. James rose also. He shook hands with the Chief, when the Chief offered his hand.

James left to begin his rounds. Mark and David followed him out to the patrol car.

Mark looked at him, curiously. He had never seen James so distracted. "Are we in trouble?" Mark asked.

James shook his head. "No, the Chief wanted to let me know about the press conference next Tuesday," said James.

"I already heard about it," said Mark.

"Well, it seems, I will be getting my Captain rank at the same time," remarked James.

"Isn't that quite a jump?" asked Mark.

"It seems, the Chief has been getting rank for me and holding it so I couldn't turn it down," explained James.

Mark thought about it for a minute, and then he started laughing.

James looked at him. "What's so funny?" he demanded.

"The Chief sure knows you," explained Mark. James looked sheepish. "Congratulations," offered Mark.

"Congratulations," said David, from the back seat.

"Thanks," James answered both. "Don't say anything until I get a chance to tell Cindy. I proposed last night and she said 'yes.'"

"Congratulations, again. I wish you both the best. I think you have a head start. You have each other," said Mark with a big smile.

"Yes, we do," agreed James.

When James signed out for lunch, he stopped at a jewelry store. Mark and David accompanied him when he went inside.

"Don't you think you ought to wait and take Cindy with you to pick out a ring?" asked Mark.

"Maybe," agreed James. "I just want to look first."

He wandered around the counter and looked at the different rings. He spotted a set he liked, but it looked expensive, so he wandered on. The clerk finished up with a customer and approached James.

"Can I help you?" she asked.

"I'm just looking around," said James.

She saw where James was looking, and decided he was looking at engagement rings. She pulled a tray from under the counter and set it on top, in front of James. "These wedding sets are discounted. Their styles have been discontinued. They are still expensive, but not as much as they were."

James looked at the sets. One set caught his eye. It was a beautiful engagement ring, with a matching wedding band for the bride and one for the groom.

"Could you put this set aside until I can bring my fiancé by to see it?" he asked.

"Sure," she said. She took the set and put his name on it and put it under the counter.

"Thanks," said James.

James, Mark, and David left to find some lunch. What James did not know was the clerk's brother had been in trouble three years before. James helped him and kept him out of jail. Her brother was now into his second year at college. The clerk went into the back and talked to the owner of the jewelry store, who just happened to be her father. She explained about James looking for wedding rings. Her father went and looked at the rings James picked out. He took the price tag out and put a new price tag on the set. The new price tag was $1000 less than the old tag.

The girl smiled at her father with satisfaction. It felt good to help one of the good guys.

After work, James went by the gallery. He asked Cindy to ride with him. He told her they would come back for her car. Cindy agreed, and James took her to the jewelry store.

When the clerk saw James come in with a young lady, she came and drew his rings from under the counter. She placed them in front of Cindy.

"Hi, Janis," said Cindy.

"Hi, Cindy, I had no idea you were Officer Michaels' fiancée," she said. "Congratulations to you both."

"Thank you," answered Cindy and James.

Cindy looked at the rings. "Oh, they are beautiful. I love them, James."

"Try on the engagement ring. See if it fits."

Cindy tried on the ring. It fit perfectly. She took it back off and handed it to James. He looked puzzled.

"Don't you like it?" he asked.

"I love it," responded Cindy. "You have to put it on my finger."

She held out her hand and James slid the ring on her finger. She threw her arms around him and held him tightly while they kissed.

Janis waited, patiently until they turned back to her. James handed her his card and she took the other rings and packaged them while she rang up his order.

When she handed him his receipt and the other rings, James glanced at the receipt. He looked startled. "I thought these rings cost more than this," he murmured. Cindy was over by the window admiring her ring.

"I told you it was on sale," replied Janis.

James shrugged. "Thank you," he said.

"Come back anytime," replied Janis.

When they went by to pick up her car, Cindy had to run in and show Melanie her ring. James went with her and stood by, patiently, while there were oohs and ahhs over the ring They decided to take her car home and go out to celebrate. James had called earlier in the day and made a reservation at one of the nicer restaurants in town. As soon as he gave his name to the greeter, they were shown to a table.

Cindy sighed, as she looked around. It was a lovely place. "You really didn't have to do this," she said.

"I know," replied James. "I'm only going to get engaged once. I want to do it right. You do like this place, don't you?"

"I love it." replied Cindy. "I just don't want you to think you have to make a habit of going to places like this. I would be just as happy curled up in your arms on the sofa at home."

James leaned across the table and kissed her. When he leaned back to his side of the table, he told Cindy about the commendation he would be receiving on Tuesday.

Cindy squeezed his hand. "I am so happy for you. You deserve it."

"Well, that's not all," said James. He proceeded to tell her about his talk with the Chief, and about all of his promotions.

"How could he do it?" asked Cindy. "Doesn't an increase in salary come with each promotion?"

James shrugged. "I just thought I was getting pay increases. I never thought about them being connected to promotions."

"Are you interested in the Captain's job when the Chief retires?" she asked.

"Not right now, but when we have children, I might like a safer job," he replied.

Cindy smiled. "I just want you to be happy. Whatever you want to do is fine with me, and I am looking forward to getting started on those children with you."

James grinned and held her hands tightly. "Me, too," he agreed.

"I have been thinking about where we are going to live when we are married," said Cindy.

"I have been thinking about it, too," said James. "My place is larger and has a larger yard. If you don't like it, we can sell both places and look for something else."

"I love your place. I think it would be a great place to raise a family. We can sell my place and use the money to fix up whatever needs fixing on yours, and, also for designing a nursery," agreed Cindy.

"I like the way you think," agreed James.

They both turned as the food was brought to the table. They set about enjoying their meal and toasting each other with a glass of champagne.

# CHAPTER 16

One month later, Cindy and James had a great time at Angelica and Alex's wedding. Mark and David were also there. Cindy had asked Angelica if she could bring David along. Angelica had assured her that he would be very welcome.

Marsha returned to town and resigned her job. She packed up, sold her house and moved to Kansas. Before she left, Cindy finished her display for the gold mirror. It was a piece of wood, painted gold, with a place in the center to attach the mirror. There was a place on each end to put screws. It could be attached to a counter or table so it could not be taken. The sign on it said "Love's Reflection Is Golden". Under it was, "Girls look in the mirror you may see the reflection of true love looking back at you." Marsha loved it and was very pleased to take it to Kansas with her.

James and Mark received their commendations and James received his new rank. Now they were at the high school where David was about to read his paper to the assembly. When his teacher read his paper, she decided everyone should hear it. She invited David's family, The Judge, the

Captain and the officers he was assigned to. She also invited the local newspaper.

James, Cindy, and Mark were seated in the front row along with the Mayor and the rest of David's family. The Judge and the Captain were in the second row behind them. David peeped through the curtains at the crowd. He was very nervous. The teacher touched him on his shoulder.

"Don't worry, you are going to be fine," she assured him.

David waited to be introduced. He then took his place at the podium.

He cleared his throat and looked at the audience. He glanced down at his paper and began to read.

"Being a police officer is not just about the law. It is about the people in the community who need the assurance of someone they can depend on in their time of need. It is about helping someone down on their luck to find a home and their dignity. It is about saving a small kitten from drowning and finding it a home. It is about helping a small crying child to be safe and finding her favorite toy. It is about helping boys on the verge of adulthood to know they can be better. A police officer reflects his love of his community out into the community, and the love is reflected back to him from a community that loves and respects him and his job. This month has shown me a new perspective on my community and its people. I will be forever grateful to Captain James Michaels and Officer Mark Black Feather for giving me this opportunity."

When David stopped, there was thunderous applause. David flushed as he came down to meet his family and friends. The local paper printed David's speech in its entirety. The story was picked up by the wire services. The story soon spread all over the country.

The next morning, as the Governor sat down to have his

morning coffee and read his newspaper, he saw the story. It was entitled "Love's Reflections." After reading the story, the Governor called his Secretary. He told his Secretary to arrange for David and his family to visit the Capitol as soon as possible.

# ABOUT THE AUTHOR

With five children, ten grandchildren and six great-grandchildren I have a very busy life, but reading and writing have always been a very large and enjoyable part of my life. I have been writing since I was very young. I kept notebooks, with my stories in them private. I didn't share them with anyone. They were all hand written because I was unable to type. We lived in the country and I had to do most of my writing at night. My days were busy helping with my brothers and sister. I also helped Mom with the garden and canning food for our family. Even though I was tired, I still managed to get my thoughts down on paper at night.

When I married and began raising my family, I continued writing my stories while helping my children through school and into their own lives and families. My sister was the only one to read my stories. She was very encouraging. When my youngest daughter started college, I decided to go to college myself. I had taken my GED at an earlier date and only had to take a class to pass my college entrance tests. I passed with flying colors and even managed to get a partial scholarship. I took computer classes to learn typing. The English language and literature classes helped me to polish my stories.

I found public speaking was not for me. I was much more comfortable with the written word, but researching and writing the speeches was helpful. I could use information to build a story. I still managed to put my own spin on the essays.

I finished college with an associate degree and a 3.4 GPA. I won several awards including President's list, Dean's list, and Faculty list. The school experience helped me gain more confidence in my writing. I want to thank my English teacher in college for giving me more confidence in my writing by telling me that I had a good imagination. She said I told an interesting story. My daughter, who is a very good writer and has books of her own published, convinced me to have some of my stories published. She published them for me. The first time I held one of my books in my hands and looked at my name on it as author, I was so proud. They were very well received. This was encouragement enough to convince me to continue writing and publishing. I have been building my library of books written by Betty McLain since then. I have also written and illustrated several children's books.

Being able to type my stories opened up a whole new world for me. Having access to a computer helped me to look up anything I needed to know and expanded my ability to keep writing my books. Joining Facebook and making friends all over the world expanded my outlook considerably. I was able to understand many different lifestyles and incorporate them in my ideas.

I have heard the saying, watch out what you say and don't make the writer mad, you may end up in a book, being eliminated. It is true. All of life is there to stimulate your imagination. It is fun to sit and think about how a thought can be changed to develop a story, and to watch the story develop and come alive in your mind. When I get started, the stories almost write themselves, I just have to get all of it down as I think of it before it is gone.

I love knowing the stories I have written are being read and enjoyed by others. It is awe-inspiring to look at the books and think 'I wrote that'.

I look forward to many more years of putting my stories out there and hope the people reading my books are looking forward as much to reading them.

Lightning Source UK Ltd.
Milton Keynes UK
UKHW022150261020
372285UK00006B/928